# Making Waves

Look out for these other titles in the

# ANGELS UNLIMITED series

www.angelsunlimited.co.uk

# Making Waves

## ANNIE DALTON

Collins

*An imprint of* HarperCollins*Publishers*

*This book is for Michael Cooke, who showed me
Cockpit Country and helped me to imagine wicked
Port Royal and the Black River Morass. Grateful
thanks to Curdella Forbes and Nadi Edwards for
recommending books, and a big thank you to Maria
for sharing her brilliant ideas!*

First published in Great Britain by Collins 2003
Collins is an imprint of HarperCollins*Publishers* Ltd,
77-85 Fulham Palace Road, Hammersmith,
London W6 8JB

The HarperCollins website address is
www.**fire**and**water**.com

1 3 5 7 9 8 6 4 2

Text copyright © Annie Dalton 2003

The author asserts the moral right to be
identified as the author of this work.

ISBN 0 00 712989 0

Printed and bound in England by
Clays Ltd, St Ives plc

# CHAPTER ONE

I miss heaps of things about my old life. Funny little things, like the smell of the face cream Mum uses last thing at night. Then there's the major stuff, like not being around to see my little sister grow up. Some days I miss Jade so badly, I'd willingly walk over burning coals to be with her for just one hour.

But you know one thing I really don't miss at ALL?

All that *posing* humans feel they have to do! Why do people DO that? Nobody really wants to be a fraud, do they? I know I didn't. Deep down I was desperate for my mates to like me just the way I was: bad habits, impossible dreams and all. Yet I kept up this big act, like I only cared about airhead stuff – style makeovers and shopping – and I wouldn't recognise a deep thought if it bit me on the bum. WHY? Why didn't I give my friends the chance to know the real Melanie Beeby?

I was just too scared basically. After my dad walked out, I didn't have much faith in the real Melanie. (Kids think it's their fault, don't they?) So I invented a new improved personality to hide behind. Like, "I'm so sassy. I'm the princess of cool!"

But kids weren't designed to fake their way through life, and a couple of weeks before my thirteenth birthday, the cracks began to show.

The weather was foul this particular day, absolutely chucking it down, and my step-dad, Des, had offered me a lift to school. Unfortunately we got stuck at some roadworks. We got stuck so long, it would have been quicker to crawl to school on my hands and knees. Suddenly I started stressing. You know, REALLY stressing. Telling myself I was going to be late again and this time it wasn't even my fault. Telling myself I was stupid to stay up half the night, making elaborate birthday invitations for my friends. Friends who didn't really care. Friends who didn't actually know me.

The thought of faking it through my own birthday celebrations just finished me off. I quickly stared out of the window, but little gasping sounds must have given me away.

I felt Des put a clean tissue in my hand. "It's going to be OK," he said quietly. "One of these days you'll find a real soul-mate, and you'll never look back."

And without any warning, I was suddenly in the middle of this HUGE mystical experience! The gridlocked lorries belching toxic fumes, the giant diggers and earth movers, the workmen in their shiny rain slickers, the little plastic bags tumbling about in the wind, all started to shimmer with otherworldly light.

"Omigosh!" I breathed. "I didn't know this world was so beautiful!"

A workman gave me a cheeky smile, and flipped his sign to read GO. The traffic queue started moving. The magical glow slowly faded, and I started feeling just a little bit silly. I decided it must have been a trick of the light. I wasn't actually convinced that deep stuff like immortal souls or Good and Evil really existed.

They do, as I was just about to find out!

The day after my birthday, I'd arranged to go shopping with my mates. My birthday cash was burning a hole in my pocket, and I was desperate to buy – I forget what, exactly. It's irrelevant anyway. Angel HQ, a.k.a. the Agency, had made other plans...

One minute I was crossing the street, humming a carefree tune, then BANG! I was soaring through the air like a swallow, skimming over rooftops, whooshing through clouds, and not only was I not showing signs of slowing down, I risked being singed by passing meteorites!

I was having my first Out of Body Experience. Not to beat about the bush, I was seriously dead. A joyrider had knocked me down in the street. No doubt this was all part of some massive heavenly design which I'll never entirely understand. Celestial personnel would have been watching over me for days. Quite probably they were in the car, when I was having my pre-birthday wobbles. The Agency never lets anyone die alone. They're v. strict on that point.

But like most humans, I had rather fixed ideas about what happens to the recently deceased. Since I didn't meet up with a dead relative, or zoom down a tunnel towards the Light, the D-word never entered my head! I just thought the usual scientific laws had been suspended for some reason. Why else would I be skimming through space as gracefully as I flew in dreams as a little kid?

I could hear strange and lovely sounds, like the throbbing of a huge invisible humming top. When I hear them now, I know I've come home. But to the old Mel Beeby, home meant a two-bedroomed flat on a housing estate. Not a vast glittering void, filled with cosmic sound FX.

Then BAM! I was set down on solid ground. I was in a crowd of chatty teenagers, heading towards a pair of tall, very swanky gates. On the other side was what seemed like a posh high school.

Of course, by this time I'm totally reeling. I'm like, what on EARTH am I doing here! Then I saw the view. And you know what? *It wasn't Earth.*

An exotic cityscape flashed and shimmered in the morning light: soaring glass skyscrapers, sparkling golden domes, curved roofs that looked almost airborne. It was like a city in the most wonderful dream you ever had. But I had the disturbing feeling that I wasn't dreaming.

Everything seemed so alive. Even the light was more super-alive than the kind I was used to. And the air! When I breathed in, I went tingly from head to toe. It smelled *wonderful* – almost, but not quite, like lilacs.

But the sign outside the school gates sent me into a spin of pure confusion.

## The Angel Academy

I told myself it was just a wussy name. It didn't mean this was a school for actual angels. And OK, so these kids looked incredibly happy and confident. And OK, so they all had a rather unusual radiant glow. They probably just had excellent skin-care regimes.

Isn't that completely classic! I'm standing like six inches away from the Pearly Gates, furiously trying to convince myself I'm not in Heaven!!

Sometimes I think I'd still be standing there, but just then another glowing girl hurried past with her mates. Everything about this girl was familiar. Her glossy black curly hair, her tough-girl walk, the sparky intelligence in her eyes.

And for the first time in years I did something that was NOT typical Melanie. I actually followed this fabulously cool person through the gates.

The two of us kind of fell into step. Not intentionally. It just seemed to happen. We kept exchanging astonished glances. Like, what IS going on here?

"Do I *know* you?" I blurted out suddenly.

And you know what? She was thinking exactly the same thing!

That's how I met my soul-mate, Lola Sanchez, Lollie to her friends.

Relax! I know what you're thinking, but no, a person does NOT normally have to die to find friends. This is basically a friendly universe, OK? Great mates can turn up anywhere and everywhere; even my old hellhole comprehensive.

But until the shock of being blasted out of my old life opened my eyes, I didn't know this. Plus, and this is pretty crucial, I didn't actually know how to BE a friend. I just knew how to fake it.

Luckily I was so shocked by my own death that for one life-changing moment, I forgot to pretend. This sparky stranger seemed like a long-lost part of me, and I wasn't about to let her vanish!

It probably sounds as if I'm just telling you how Lola and I met up, as some kind of ice-breaker, before zooming on to something more major. I'm not. The fact is I desperately need you to understand why Lola is so special to me.

Listen, that girl has loads of friends. Lola is a friend magnet! Yet from my first day at the Angel Academy, she made it her business to be there for me – yes, ME! Day after day, this hugely popular girl was encouraging me to do my best, letting me cry on her shoulder when I'd made yet another cosmic boo-boo, and booting me back out into the Universe to try again and again. Now that's true friendship, right?

It was Lola who finally taught me I didn't have to fake it to be popular. "Melanie, I have met teeny-weeny *worms* with better opinions of themselves," she sighed. "So your papa left you. That was harsh, girl. But get over it, you're in Heaven now. Time to lose that airhead disguise!"

Lola had only known me a few days when she said that, and already she knew me better than I knew myself! And this girl and I had SO much in common. Which is insane, since Lollie originally comes from the twenty-second century! Yet we had the same mad sense of humour, we loved almost exactly the same styles of music. And we regularly borrowed each other's clothes.

I felt so lucky it almost scared me. And it wasn't too long before I had a totally good reason to feel this way.

Our history group had been doing this huge project on ancient Egypt. Our teacher, Mr Allbright, decided it would be helpful to experience the vibes for ourselves. Omigosh, the hassle we had on that trip!! Not to mention the *dust*! The instant we got back, Lola and I dashed back to our dorms and showered like demons.

Now I was catching up on homey chores: watering my thirsty baby orange tree, checking through my post. Lola was sitting on my bed in her PJs, writing up her report.

Before she died and became an angel, my soul-mate lived in a vibey third-world city. Lollie herself is a mix of a dozen different nationalities: Portuguese, Dutch, African. She even has Mayan ancestry – can you believe that? Her granny told her that's where she got her great cheekbones!

I glanced across at this amazing girl and I thought how we would never even have met if it wasn't for a total miracle. (No, trust me. Mel Beeby winning a cosmic scholarship is a miracle!)

All at once I felt this pang of – I don't know – *foreboding*. "Lollie, we're always going to be friends, aren't we?" I asked anxiously.

She peered at me over her little reading glasses. "What's wrong, girl? Not having a big bad premonition, are you?"

I gulped. "I was just thinking I couldn't bear it if I had to go back to that phoney person I used to be."

Lola leaned over and patted my hand. "That's not going to happen! We're soul-mates, babe. We knew each other back at the Dawn of Creation." She gave me a mysterious smile. "And I'm pretty sure we've been reunited for a reason!"

I felt a prickle of excitement. "Are you serious?"

Her eyes sparkled. "This is still like the apprenticeship stage. But once we've got through our angel warrior training, we'll be incredibly wise and strong—"

"—but in a cute way," I suggested, giggling.

"*Cute?*" Lola sniffed. "We'll be gorgeous!! We'll be such an unstoppable cosmic force, the PODS will go whimpering back to the Hell dimensions like ugly little puppy dogs!"

"You think so?" I said wistfully.

Lola's brows drew together. "Are you doubting the sacred words of La Sanchez?"

I swallowed. "Suppose we'd met on Earth? As humans I mean? Would we have recognised each other then?"

Lola looked surprised. "Sure!"

"But would we though?" I persisted. "There's so much pressure on that little planet, Lollie. Even angels can't hear themselves think."

"Hey girl, I'd know *you* anywhere! I'd feel it – in here." Lola pressed her hand to her heart. "So would you."

I was so touched I didn't know what to say.

Suddenly, Lola was completely distracted. She jumped up and turned up the volume on my radio. "I just can't get enough of this tune!" she sighed happily. "It is totally, totally luminous!"

The radio station was playing a hip-hop remix of *True Colors*. We started to sing along. Lola literally sings like an angel. I sing more like a little squeaky reptile. But it sounded OK when we sang together. It sounded nice.

But I must have been having a big bad premonition after all. Three weeks after our conversation, my soul-mate and I were torn apart, separated by something so dark, it could only have been invented in one of the Hell dimensions. Like all truly terrible things, it happened on Earth.

But it began with Brice.

# CHAPTER TWO

Sorry, I've got to interrupt the flow. I'm worried you don't understand about the war. That cosmic war I'm always on about? I'm not sure you realise how big this is.

It's MASSIVE. Battles between the two major cosmic agencies are going on in every single century in human history. This conflict gets more intense every day. Want to know what we're fighting over?

YOU.

The PODS, a.k.a. the Powers of Darkness, a.k.a. the Opposition, want total control of your souls. They want you to live your life in a kind of dreary waking dream where nothing matters because nothing feels real. They want you to forget who you are.

You think that couldn't happen, right?

You think you'd know if someone was interfering with your head?

Look, I don't have time to get into PODS strategies right now, but trust me, OK? Those guys have been around for AEONS. They know a zillion dirty tricks to play on human minds. Our school library has a ton of books devoted to that one subject alone.

My agency, on the other hand, doesn't want to own anybody's soul, thanks. We think your soul is your personal property. We do have an agenda, but it's the total opposite. We want you to wake up and remember who you really are, so you can have a fabulously rewarding time on your gorgeous little planet!

Check this – life on Earth was actually meant to be FUN.

Unfortunately, the Dark Powers have lulled millions of human beings into a state of cosmic amnesia. They've been doing it since Time began. They're *still* doing it today. Now I'm going to let you in on another celestial secret.

You are the reason the Heavenly City never sleeps. Yes – you!

When I look out of the dorm window at night, I can see brilliant star bursts of light over the Agency Tower, *FLASH*, *FLASH*, *FLASH*, about a heartbeat apart. Know what that is? Each star burst is an agent returning from, or departing to, Planet Earth. Plus we have Heaven-based agents beam uplifting vibes at you morning, noon and night. Joy, Peace, Love, whatever. Those aren't just words in Christmas carols, you know, they're powerful energy vibrations. We can actually see them on the Angel Watch computer screens, forming a beautiful web of light around your gorgeous little blue-green planet.

That's how precious humans are. That's why the Agency will never give up on you, EVER. Your family and friends might give up on you. You might even give up on yourself. Hey, your dog might give up on you! But the Heavenly City stays open for business twenty-four-seven.

Which brings me right back to Brice, one-time cosmic dropout, now humiliatingly doing retakes at the Angel Academy.

I'm not sure there is such a thing as an average angel, but if so Brice is definitely not it. The guy wears ripped T-shirts advertising bizarre celestial rock bands. He is basically a total outlaw.

What is a boy like that doing in Heaven? Ooh, good question. I could tell you he's a bad boy who sold his soul and accidentally found his heart. Or I could say he used to be a fallen angel who got homesick for the Light. But the truth is a little more complicated.

I ran into him on my first field trip to Earth, when he was working for the PODS. Technically we were cosmic enemies. Technically, Brice and I were also total strangers. Yet for reasons I won't go into, it felt like he knew me a *leetle* too well for comfort. Lola believes our meeting was some big prearranged karmic thing. She says when we met up that day in foggy 1940s' London, our souls went, "Omigosh, it's you!"

"Brice made a big mistake," Lola explained solemnly. "One day he woke up and found himself on the totally wrong side in the cosmic war. He needed to find a way back home, and you were it, girl."

Maybe, maybe not. But when the heavenly authorities finally agreed to let Brice come back to our school, I was completely disgusted. I couldn't believe I had to share Heaven with this devious dirtbag!

According to our headmaster, you see, Brice's dodgy past was all water under the bridge. Michael's theory was, if you wait long enough, trees evolve into diamonds, and bad boys come good.

At the time I'm like, yeah right, and we're all made of stardust and what's that got to do with the price of cheese?

But now I've started to wonder if there's something in this evolution stuff after all, because gradually my feelings towards Brice began to change.

It was disturbing at first, looking up in the library to see my cosmic enemy feverishly turning pages at the next table. Plus, for a boy who once hobnobbed with demons, he looked kind of vulnerable. I'd seen Brice's dangerous side, however, so I had no intention of being suckered in. But as the months passed, I started to get used to having him around.

After he came with me and Lollie to Victorian times, I began to feel almost, well, *fond* of him.

The day after we got back from ancient Egypt, Brice was slumped at the back of the class wearing shades, and a T-shirt that said ASTRAL GARBAGE.

He wasn't the only one feeling hungover that day. We'd all been humungously affected by some toxic ancient Egyptian vibes. Everyone was suffering, including Mr Allbright.

Halfway through the lesson, our teacher noticed my new Emily Strange top and went up the wall! "A garment decorated with a skull and crossbones is *not* suitable clothing for school, Melanie," he said in a shocked voice.

"I think it's sweet," I objected. "It's a sweet, fun, retro thing."

"Pirates were not sweet, Melanie. They certainly weren't fun. They were calculating, cold-blooded murderers."

Lola and I secretly hid our smiles. You see, on our trip to Elizabethan England, Lollie and I had met the sweetest pirate ever. His daughter, Cat Darcy, was in love with Shakespeare. I'm not name-dropping, it's true! Though actually, the world's most famous writer went under the name of Chance, back then. He was going through a really bad patch and Cat's pirate dad helped to straighten him out. Listen, I'm not saying piracy is cool. And I'm not saying Cat's father was a harmless pussycat. I'm just saying that even a pirate can surprise you by having a heart.

Mind you, I was pretty sure Mr Allbright knew this already. And to be fair, our teacher is not normally the type to stress over an innocent fashion statement.

He was stressing because:

- He'd been zapped by toxic vibes like everyone else, and
- We were rapidly approaching the end of term and NO ONE in our class had shown any interest in entering the HALO awards.

"I've got entry forms here," he said reproachfully at the end of the lesson. "Think about it at least."

Lola and I didn't pay too much attention. We had to dash to the library to catch up on an assignment. We'd been scribbling madly for about ten minutes, when Brice mooched around the stacks.

"Fancy skiving off?" he said in a casual voice.

Lola sighed. "Love to, babe. Unfortunately we have to do this thing."

Brice cleared his throat. "That's a shame. I had

a proposition. I was wondering if you'd both be interested in a joint entry for the HALO awards."

Lola looked puzzled. "Who with?"

He went red. "Well, me, obviously."

I couldn't believe my ears. "You are kidding!"

Brice scowled. "Is there some reason I shouldn't enter?"

"Of course not," said Lola quickly. "The awards are open to every trainee in the school."

"You've got to admit it's a bit out of character," I grinned.

I meant it as a joke, but Brice just muttered something uncomplimentary and stormed out.

Lola and I looked at each other.

"That went well," she said in a small voice.

I felt like a really bad person, but I wasn't ready to admit it. "That boy has such a major chip," I complained.

Our buddy Reuben came over. "You guys look upset."

Lola started to explain but other library users started ssshing.

"Let's go to Guru," Reuben suggested. "You can tell me there."

"Why not," Lola said bleakly. "My concentration's totally shot."

Guru is less than five minutes' walk from our school. We grabbed an outdoor table in the sun and ordered the café's special Aztec hot chocolate, otherwise known as the trainee angel's cure-all.

I think Mo, the guy who runs Guru now, sensed something was up, because when he brought our order he tactfully left extra marshmallows.

Lola was too upset to notice. "It's really hard for Brice to ask people for help," she said miserably. "And we laughed in his face."

"We did NOT laugh in his face," I objected. "We were just – surprised."

"You told him he was a phoney," Reuben pointed out.

"It was a joke, man! The guy used to live in the Hell dimensions! I can't believe he's that sensitive."

"Believe it," said Reuben.

Lola's eyes were huge with worry. "This is a really tough time for Brice, Melanie. He's on probation and everyone at our school knows it."

The extra marshmallows were going to waste so I popped two into my hot chocolate and immediately felt ashamed.

When Brice first got a scholarship to the Angel Academy, I'm sure he secretly dreamed of climbing all the way to the top of that dizzy ladder to the stars. Instead, he tripped over a monster snake and went slipping and sliding all the way back to square one. Now he was having to start his gruelling game of cosmic snakes and ladders all over again. Only this time everyone was watching...

"Winning a HALO would be like saying he was rehabilitated," Lola was saying earnestly. "He wouldn't have to spend his angelic career looking over his shoulder."

"Lollie, if this was me, you'd tell me to get over it."

She patted my hand. "True! But if you asked us to back you, we'd do it like a shot. We wouldn't even think about it."

I felt myself go all emotional. "Really?"

My mates nodded vigorously.

A worry slid into my mind. "You don't think this was a test? Like Brice was checking to see if we're really his friends?"

Reuben winced. "Actually—"

"Omigosh!" I wailed. "I feel *terrible*. Now he's

going to think we've been faking. We've got to go and find him."

"Too obvious," Reuben advised. "He'd hate it if he knew we'd been talking about him. Bring it up casually next time you see him."

"Why do *I* have to bring it up?" I whinged. "Why can't Lola?"

She went pink. "Because it would be better coming from you."

I got my chance that night at the Babylon Café.

The Babylon is our fave place to go dancing. They have the best live music ever. But if you want to cool off or just chill with your mates, you can go outside into their magical gardens. They're designed so they literally seem suspended in midair. At night they're all lit up with twinkly white lights.

I'd gone out for some air when I spotted Brice in the shadows, watching the dancers. It was a warm night, but he wore his jacket collar turned up, and his hands were jammed into his pockets. Somehow Brice was always on the outside, looking in. The thought gave me a funny pang in my heart, because I remember how that feels.

I took a deep breath and went up to him. "Hi."

"Nice dress." There was absolutely no expression in his voice.

"Thanks. About this morning—"

Brice's jaw muscles tensed. "It was a dumb idea."

"It wasn't. I was tired and crabby. I wasn't thinking."

He shrugged. "Whatever."

I almost stamped with frustration. "Could you just listen?"

"*You* listen, sweetheart," he blazed. "You were right the first time. I am not the HALO type."

"There isn't a HALO type, fool! That's what I'm trying to tell you. I'd love to enter the awards with you."

"Yeah, right," he jeered. "I saw how you both rushed to sign up."

"I mean it! I've never won anything in my entire existence. OK, at my old school, I won a box of cheap chocs in a raffle. But I've never won an actual *award*. It'd be cool to win a HALO, like getting an angel Oscar."

Brice scowled. "Is that the speech? Will you stop bugging me now?"

"No, actually," I said sweetly. "I'm going to keep bugging you until you tell me what we have to do to enter."

There was an interesting silence while Brice chewed at his lip.

"Well for a start, we fill in the forms," he said cautiously. "The HALO judges might not accept us. They don't always."

"They will! I know they will!" I bubbled. "Oh, this is SO great! Let's do it first thing tomorrow."

"If you want," he shrugged. "It's really no biggie."

Liar, I thought. This was obviously HUGE for Brice. I could tell he still felt really bruised.

You know that thing? The bimbo thing that I'm not meant to do any more? I think maybe I do it because I don't know what else TO do.

I looked at him under my lashes. "Brice, how do HALOs work at high-school level exactly? At the angel nursery where I help out, kids are doing really cute projects."

"Maybe you didn't notice, but I don't do 'cute'," he said with distaste. "We'd be in the advanced section, darling."

I knew he was thawing slightly, so I did another

Bambi-eyed flutter. "I still don't quite understand," I said innocently. "What would we have to do?"

"We have to go on a blind date with destiny."

"Omigosh! Tell me more!" I giggled.

I know, I know, I should have more pride. But hey, it worked.

"We volunteer for an unknown mission," Brice explained. "The HALO panel put their heads together to discuss our various strengths and weaknesses. On that basis, they decide what cosmic experiences are likely to stretch us and take us to the next angelic level, yadda yadda."

"Yadda yadda," I echoed, to show I was keeping up.

"They pick a suitable time and place, and off we go."

"Sounds like a huge challenge," I said in my most impressed voice.

"I think that's the general idea," said Brice. "Evolution and all that."

"Well, definitely count me in, babe."

"What about Lola? Is she in too?"

"Oh, I really couldn't say," I said innocently. "You'll have to ask her."

He grinned. "Yeah right! Like you two don't discuss *everything*!"

I blushed. Brice definitely wouldn't want me to know about the night he and Lola got all romantic under the stars last holidays!

"Oh, look! Lollie's over there by the fountains!" I exclaimed with relief. "Ask her yourself."

Brice sauntered over. I saw him and Lola deep in conversation through veils of falling water.

Yess! My ploy had worked!

I know, I know! I'm in Heaven now. I should drop the airhead disguise, but sometimes it comes in SO useful!!

The judges did accept our entry as I somehow knew they would.

But now it's confession time. On the day Mr Allbright was due to announce our time destinations for the HALO, I had genuinely good intentions. No, I really did! I was all set to take notes and ask questions. And believe me, I truly wish I had.

But when our teacher told us we'd be going to seventeenth-century Jamaica, everything else flew out of my head. I practically went into orbit!! I'm like, "Woo! I am SO packing my bikini!"

I literally didn't hear another word anyone said!

I'd always felt a mysterious connection with Jamaica. Some of my friends at my old earth school told me how amazing it was, and I'd dream about going to see it for myself. But this was going to be SO much better! We were going to time-travel to this gorgeous tropical island, *centuries* before the tourist invasion. We'd see the island of Jamaica in its original unspoilt state!

I'd have loved to stay and chat about our mysterious Caribbean mission with my HALO team-mates, but all three of us had appointments elsewhere. Lola had a singing lesson. Brice trudged off for his weekly chat with our headmaster, one of the conditions of his probation. And I help out at the angel nursery school most Wednesday afternoons.

I flew back to our dorm to change. I burst into my room, still buzzing with excitement and caught sight of myself in the mirror. I was clutching an official-looking Agency folder.

"I don't believe it!" I wailed. "This is so unfair!"

I'd been so busy daydreaming about tropical sunshine, I hadn't noticed Mr Allbright give out our bios for the mission. An angel only needs a cover story if she's going to be visible.

I could forget the cute bikini. Chances were I'd be going to Jamaica in a corset!! But like Reuben says, "Angels gotta take the yin with the yang." I decided that wearing a corset would be a really small price to pay for a working holiday on a paradise island.

When I got to the nursery school, the children were just finishing their yoga practice. They looked so-o sweet, sitting in the lotus position on their little pink mats! I have learned such a lot from those angel babies. They can be incredibly wise. They can also be incredibly naughty!

Their rehearsal for the preschool HALO show was a riot. Afterwards I helped Miss Dove clear up. "Thank you for helping, Melanie," she said warmly. "I know the children are hoping you'll come and help on the big day. Friday isn't your usual day for coming in, but do you think you could make it?"

Being appreciated makes you feel all warm and fuzzy, doesn't it? When I feel like that, I'd do anything for anyone.

"Wouldn't miss it for the world," I beamed.

Next morning I woke with a bloodcurdling shriek.

I'd only promised to help Miss Dove on the same day we were due to fly out to seventeenth-century Jamaica!

If it was anyone else but those little angel kids, I'd have pulled a Houdini and wiggled out of it. But I owed them big time. I'd had some dark times when I first got here and Miss Dove and her preschoolers saved my sanity. I was desperately disappointed, but I didn't feel like I had a choice.

Someone would have to take my place on the HALO mission.

I just hoped Brice would understand.

## CHAPTER THREE

Two hours later I was sitting on a patch of daisies outside the school library, sobbing my heart out. Reuben had tactfully brought me outside before I made a total fool of myself.

"I said there was still time to get someone else," I hiccupped, "and he just went ballistic! He said I had *ruined* his chances of getting a HALO!"

"He's upset," Reuben said calmly. "He's having one of those cosmic wobbles like we all do."

I hunted for a fresh tissue. "Brice has wobbles?" I sniffled. "I don't think so."

"Mel, get real! The guy's only been back in Heaven a few months. When he came back his clothes still reeked of sulphur, remember?"

I blew my nose. "I know. Lola had to take him shopping," I remembered. "He's been through stuff I can't even imagine."

"Ssh, it's going to be OK." Reuben was rubbing my back in soothing circles. Unlike me and Lola, Reubs is pure angel, and though he doesn't look particularly tough, he has this inner strength that comes from having grown up in the angel bizz.

"I don't know what to do, Reubs!" I wept.

Reuben thought for a moment. "What does Helix say?" Helix is my official angel name. It's a really big moment when a trainee gets his or her true angel name. But Helix is also like, my inner angel, and I'm meant to tune into her when things get rough. Unfortunately, when things get rough I find it hard to believe I even HAVE an inner angel.

"You tell me," I choked. "You're the angel. I'm just a – a faker!"

He laughed. "Rubbish. Your inner angel is always online."

"If you say so," I snuffled. "But I'm going to feel really stupid when nothing happens."

I shut my eyes and took slow, deep breaths. The

Angel Handbook said it was hard to connect with your inner angel if you were upset. After a few minutes, the centre of my chest began to feel like I'd swallowed a tiny hot potato and it was still trapped halfway down. It seemed as if Helix was keen to get in touch with me too.

When I opened my eyes some time later I felt stunned. "Helix says Brice needs me. He and Lola both need me on this mission."

"Problem solved," said Reuben cheerfully.

I sighed. "What she didn't say, is how I can be in two places at once!"

My buddy rolled his eyes. "Duh! Remind me what that big A on your jacket stands for again?"

"I know! I'm an angel! Tell me how that helps?"

"You're a celestial being, Melanie! Time is not a problem."

"It isn't?" I said hopefully.

Apparently it wasn't. Reuben suggested a v. sensible alternative scenario. Lola and Brice would go ahead as planned. I'd keep my promise to my baby angels, jump into my seventeenth-century corset, sprint down to the Agency, catch the first available portal and join the others in the sun. Sorted!

"The time technicians will get you there a few hours after Lollie and Brice at most."

I was stunned. "You're a genius!"

"Thanks," Reuben said modestly. "You'd better tell Brice, so Mr Allbright can make arrangements."

"Brice could have told me this," I said suddenly.

Reuben gave me a lopsided smile. "I expect he thought you knew."

I went cold. Brice didn't realise I was being dense. He thought I was fobbing him off with any old excuse. He thought I genuinely didn't want to go!

"Sorry, gotta go!" I said urgently. "Later, Reubs."

I went hunting for him all over the campus, but Brice had totally gone to ground. Just as I'd given up all hope I saw a familiar figure in an outsized hoodie trudging out through the gates.

"Brice – wait!!"

He waited with a bored expression.

Trust me, no one does "bored" like Brice. He's like a porcupine, always putting up sharp prickles. But I told myself I wasn't going to let him get to me. This time I'd get it right.

"I've, erm, just been talking to Reuben," I began.

"And I should care because?"

And BOSH! My good intentions went out the window just like that!

"You should care, you thick bozo, because Reuben reminded me I'm a celestial being. Which means I could be on your HALO team, assuming you still want me. So do you or don't you? I haven't got all day, you know!" I was literally yelling into his face.

Brice looked genuinely shocked. "You're being unusually forceful."

"Yes, I am," I snapped. "I'm sick of tiptoeing round you, like you've got some fatal disease, you moron."

He gave a startled grin. "That's a fine way for a celestial being to address another celestial being!"

I glared at him. "OK, then: jerk, creep, dirtbag. Take your pick."

The grin vanished. "Your point being?"

"My point being that real friends don't tiptoe round each other."

There was an electrifying pause.

"Friends?" Brice repeated.

I smiled down at my shoes. "Obviously there's still a way to go. But if trees can turn into diamonds, anything's possible, right?"

I could feel Brice looking at the top of my head. "OK, Mel Beeby, future friend," he said softly. "What's the game plan?"

Confession time. No, really, BIG confession time.

I TRULY intended to read my bio. The night before our mission, I actually curled up in my uncomfortable school armchair and opened the first page, but then Lola popped her head round the door to see if I fancied a takeaway. She hadn't read her bio either. So we both went into total denial mode and ordered this massive feast from the Silver Lychee! A bit naughty I know, but their food is SO-O delicious!

Over our meal, my friend and I got into this really deep conversation and before we knew it, the evening had flown by.

Eventually, Lola started collecting up takeaway cartons.

"*Hey, carita!* We didn't do our fortune cookies!"

"We can do them now!" I said, stifling my yawns.

Lola's fortune said she was going to risk everything for love. Mine said I would have to learn to tell the real from the unreal.

"How come I never get to fall in love?" I moaned.

I could weep when I remember us innocently reading our cookie fortunes. If we'd shared our bios then, things might have been so different. But I started on about my stupid corset and that led into happy reminiscences about Shakespeare's girlfriend.

"Cat Darcy had it all," Lola sighed. "She was pretty, smart, brave."

"It must have been a nightmare being a black person in England then. The Elizabethans treated her like she was some exotic pet."

"Chance didn't," Lola said softly. "Shakespeare, I mean."

"Those two were true soul-mates, weren't they?"

"I wanted them to get it together, didn't you?"

"Totally. But if Chance had gone to sea like Cat's dad suggested, he'd never have discovered he was a play-writing genius."

Lola did one of those stretches that makes her look just like a cat. "Gotta move my angel booty," she yawned. "Brice is picking me up in two hours."

I gave her a hug. "Watch out for the Caribbean love-interest."

"And you go on keeping it real, girlfriend!"

I heard Lola pattering down the hall in her little beaded slippers, and the soft double clunk as her door opened and closed.

Next morning there was a note pinned to my door: Soul-mates see each other's true colours, no matter what. Big love 2U, Lollie

It was like she knew.

A few minutes before I was due at the nursery school, I finally glanced through my bio. I couldn't see too much to worry about. The character in my cover story even shared my real first name to my relief.

Melanie Woodhouse had grown up in England, but her parents had died and she'd been sent to Jamaica to live with her uncle and aunt. They were called Josiah and Sarah Bexford and owned a sugar plantation with the magic name of Fruitful Vale.

This is going to be SO sublime, I sighed happily. I was OK with being visible now. For one thing, when you're visible you can enjoy the local food. Once my friend Lateesha's mum cooked this massive Jamaican Sunday brunch for us. Ohhh! It made my mouth water to think of it.

When I got to the nursery, everyone was outside in the sun. Chairs were set out in rows for specially invited guests. Our headmaster was in the front row, chatting to Miss Dove. At least he was trying to! Several overexcited preschoolers had decided to use him as a climbing frame.

Michael seems so human and easy-going, it's easy to forget he's an archangel; until you look into his eyes. Omigosh, those scary-beautiful eyes just see right into your soul!

"Melanie!" he said warmly. "I hope you're going to sit next to me! It's been too long."

"Hey, who's fault is that? I turn up every day!"

It's a standing school joke that our headmaster is almost never around. As archangel with special responsibility for Earth, Michael is constantly jetting off to historical trouble spots. Yet here he was, keen to see the little nursery school angels do their stuff, looking slightly tired but totally serene.

Preschool angels obviously can't go off on dangerous missions. But they're desperate to do their bit for the Universe. Miss Dove wanted to encourage this positive attitude, so she'd arranged for them to perform their HALO contributions in front of a friendly heavenly audience.

The children had been practising for WEEKS. The Rose group performed last of all, looking totally darling in their miniature school casuals. They'd organised (you're not going to believe this!) a Giggle Marathon!

I'd already seen them in rehearsal, but it got me every time. There's something about preschool angels laughing. They sound SO naughty!

Soon everyone in the audience was laughing helplessly. Michael totally couldn't stop. He even set Miss Dove off and she is the soul of professionalism, believe me.

Finally the children took their bow, still giggling. Some of them could hardly stand by this time!

"Thank you," Michael told them, wiping his eyes. "Who'd like to tell me about this unusual project?"

One of my favourite preschoolers stepped forward. Obi has absolutely no hair, almost invisible eyebrows, and the calmest face you have ever seen. He looks just like a mini Buddha.

"Miss Dove said to think of a project that could make Earth a happier place," Obi said shyly. "So Maudie said we should just giggle and have fun. She said our vibes will beam all the way to Earth and children will catch them and start giggling and feel happy again."

"Is that right, Maudie?" Michael asked gently. "Was this your idea?"

She gave him an awed nod. "Yes, because giggling is catching. When I start I can't ever stop."

There was a kiddies' party afterwards. Unfortunately, I only had time to grab a fairy cake before I had to leave.

I was SO touched when Michael offered to take me down to the Agency and see me off.

"I'm glad you felt able to support Brice's HALO entry," he said as we purred downtown in his awesome Agency car. "This one could be quite a challenge for you all."

"Oh, we're old hands now. We'll be fine!" I said airily.

No matter what time you go, it's always crowded in Departures. I rushed into the ladies' cloakroom and came out feeling self-conscious in my seventeenth-century cap and gown.

One thing I find so comforting, is the way the Agency gets every teensy historical detail just right.

Like the coin purse hanging at my waist had items of real seventeenth-century jewellery in it. Nothing flash. Just the type of sweet simple trinkets my character would have.

Michael and I joined the long queue for angel tags. No one is allowed to leave Heaven without them. They basically tell the Universe that we're on official business, plus they keep us in touch with all the angelic support guys.

I saw a sudden flicker of worry in Michael's eyes. He'd seen my teacher talking to a junior agent. "Excuse me, Melanie, we may have a problem." Michael hurried over to Mr Allbright.

I had a bad feeling in the pit of my stomach. I caught confused snatches of their conversation. Communications between Heaven and Earth had been disrupted in the early hours, only seconds after two trainees left on a HALO mission.

I knew it had to be Brice and Lola.

I heard Michael say, "And there's been no word? Well, page me as soon as you hear anything."

The agent hurried away. Michael and Mr Allbright went into a huddle but this time I couldn't hear what they said.

I'd collected my tags. Now I didn't know what to

do. I glanced up to find Al, my favourite maintenance man, at my side.

"Your portal's ready, doll, but it looks like we've got a bit of a situation," he said sympathetically.

Michael and Mr Allbright came over, looking really grim.

"I'm calling your mission off," Michael said bluntly. "We're fairly sure your friends arrived in the right time slot, but unusual atmospheric conditions are making it impossible to pick up signals. Mr Allbright and I have considered various options and decided to send in a SWAT team."

"To get them back? No way!" The words burst out before I'd even thought. "It's the worst thing you could do!"

Michael looked startled. "Melanie, we're trying to save him."

"Yeah, save his hide, but what about Brice's self-respect? He'd think he was a major loser. You've got to let him sort this out on his own."

Mr Allbright had joined us. "This is not about doubting Brice's ability," he said quietly.

"Oh, really! What is it about then?" I was fuming.

He sighed. "It's about the school acting responsibly."

"You're wrong," I said angrily. "You're not seeing the big picture."

Michael took a breath. "Your friends could be at risk. I've decided to bring them home. That's all there is to it."

"NO! Whatever it is, Brice and Lola can deal with it. Why won't you *trust* them?" I was yelling at an archangel, but I knew I was right.

"I'm sorry, Melanie," he said, "this is one for the professionals."

I was getting that burning hot-potato sensation. My inner angel wanted to get in on the discussion. "Tell the truth, babe!" she whispered. "But try not to lose your temper."

I forced myself to calm down. "Listen, everyone knows Brice and I aren't exactly bosom buddies. When he came back I was just waiting for him to screw up. The way I saw it, I was right and good, and he was bad and wrong. If he screwed up, he'd be bad for ever, and I'd be good for ever. That's how I was thinking."

"I fail to see—" Michael began.

"That's what I'm trying to TELL you! If you rush to his rescue, you're as good as telling him he's got no future as an agent!"

"On the contrary, we're showing him how much we value—"

I cut across him. "Can you see Brice doing some heavenly desk job? Omigosh, Michael! It would kill him!"

He looked upset. "Melanie, there will be other opportunities—"

"Not like this. I truly think this could be a cosmic thingummy. A turning point, kind of. Like, if Brice can get through this, he'll know he can make it in the angel bizz."

"What if he doesn't get through it?" Mr Allbright's brow was puckered with worry.

"I can't think that far," I confessed. "I just know you've got to give him a chance."

They exchanged glances.

"Excuse us," Michael murmured.

My headmaster and Mr Allbright went off into a huddle. I was so tense I was literally digging my nails into my palms. Their private conflab lasted for aeons. Mr Allbright kept shaking his head dubiously. Eventually Michael walked back to me. His expression was so grave that I felt sure it was bad news.

"Mr Allbright and I have agreed that you must do what you think is right," he said in a quiet voice.

I went weak with relief. "I promise I won't let you down."

Urgent squawking sounds came over Al's headphones. The time technicians were getting twitchy.

"Hate to hassle you people," Al said apologetically, "but we're cutting this really fine."

"Just let us have a few more seconds." Michael's scary-beautiful eyes searched mine. "I know Lola is your best friend, but I'm not sure you realise how dange—"

I shook my head. "It isn't just Lola."

"You feel responsible for Brice, is that it?"

"I think," I started shyly. "I think when Brice met me in London that time, it reminded him what he'd lost. In a funny kind of way, I'm the reason he came back to our school. He signed up for the HALO mission because I promised I'd be on his team. Now something's gone wrong." My eyes stung with tears. "I should have been there, Michael. I *have* to go."

This time Michael didn't attempt to change my mind. He simply held out his hand for my tags. "Shall I fasten those?"

He did up the clasp, and I found myself engulfed in the fizzy rainbow cloud of Michael's energy field. I literally saw light and colours whooshing everywhere! All at once, my heart was burstingly full of love. It was like the tiniest glimpse of how it might feel to be an archangel.

I tottered into my portal, still fizzing with angelic electricity.

"Take care, Melanie," Michael said softly. "Call the Agency as soon as you can."

"I will!"

"Good luck, doll," called Al.

The glass door slid shut. Al said something into his headpiece, then gave me a thumbs up. I waved to show I was ready.

We must have been cutting it REALLY fine, because next minute my portal lit up like a laser show and I was blasted out of Heaven.

Soon afterwards, I felt the familiar jolt, as the portal burst through the invisible barrier that separates the angelic fields from the human realms of Time and Space. I wasn't actually watching. I was emptying out my flight bag, desperately trying to find my bio. I'd planned to have a quick last-minute read. Omigosh, Melanie,

I scolded myself. You'd better not have left it behind!

But as it turned out, reading was not an option. Seconds later, my portal started pitching about like you would not believe. We'd hit major cosmic turbulence.

Must be those weird atmospheric conditions Michael was talking about, I thought anxiously.

I glanced through the window and was alarmed to see time zones streaming past in a multicoloured blur. We were travelling fast, even by Agency standards. Screechy metallic sounds started up under my feet. The portal began to judder. I could literally feel my back teeth vibrating.

I hit the PANIC button. "Help!" I shouted. "Get me back. We'll have to abort this mission. This thing is shaking itself to pieces!"

Weird staticky sounds came from my radio, making me clutch my ears. My radio link was malfunctioning along with everything else.

"Help!" I called again. "Al? Michael? Can anyone hear me?"

Outside, history was flashing past my eyes like colours in a migraine.

I thought I was going to dissolve with terror. Could angels actually DIE? It was one of those technical details I was always intending to look up. Now it could be too late.

"Michael, if you can hear me, please help!" I moaned. "Please, please..."

Then a jagged hole tore in the portal and I was sucked out into space.

## Chapter Four

In my dream I was lost in roaring darkness. Lightning flashes showed lurid glimpses of a terrifying dream world. FLASH! Palm trees bent almost double. FLASH! A wooden chair sailing through the air. FLASH! Water rushing – a river? A lake? And again pitch black.

The roaring, rushing nightmare went on for what seemed hours. Nothing was solid. Nothing made sense. Nothing felt real.

Then I felt gentle hands take hold of me inside my dream, lifting me up as if I weighed no more than air. I was laid on something soft and carried through the lashing wind and rain. My rescuers called to each other in a musical dream language, a language I miraculously understood.

"She is here," they told each other. "She flew here on the wings of the storm. Now the end is coming."

Another flash showed me a brief, electrifying vision: six or seven concerned faces gazing down at me through the falling rain. They wore strange ornaments made of pearls and seashells. The colours shimmered against their half-naked bodies like colours you only see in dreams...

I opened my eyes and found myself lying in a large four-poster bed. Velvet curtains had been looped back at one side. An oil lamp made silky gleams on polished wood. Everything else was in deep shadow.

There was a strange fog inside my head, making it hard to think.

I didn't know where I was. And omigosh, this was really bad. I didn't actually know *who* I was!

I heard stealthy creaks. My heart thumped like a rabbit's. Someone was in my room, and I didn't know if they were friend or foe.

"Is anyone out there?" I whimpered.

I heard more creaks as someone shifted his or her weight in a chair. Then I heard slow shuffling footsteps. An old black woman peered through my curtains. "Lawd a mercy!" she exclaimed. "You come back to us!"

I could have cried with relief. She knows who I am, I thought. Now I'll find out what's going on.

"Have I been away?" I said huskily. My throat was incredibly sore.

"You been sick, bad bad, Miss Melanie."

Miss Melanie. That had to be me. This old woman must be my nurse.

"I'm very thirsty," I croaked.

"Have a sip a dis cordial. Don't sit up too fas'," she warned.

The cool drink was blissful, but the effort of drinking wore me out. I collapsed back on my pillows, trembling.

I felt haunted by my horrible nightmare. I wasn't sure if I was truly awake, or if this was just another episode in the same dream.

Nothing seemed fixed or solid or familiar. The room, the old-fashioned bed, the tired old nurse.

I watched her from under my eyelashes, wondering what it was about her that disturbed me. Her eyes are so sad, I thought. Next minute this thought slipped away and I found myself glancing nervously into the corners of the room.

There was something creepy about those shadows. They might morph into something else when I wasn't looking. Something evil.

You're being pathetic, I told myself. You're in a big comfy bed in this lovely peaceful room. You're weak from this illness, that's all. There's absolutely nothing to be scared of.

Except that I'd lost my memory.

The old nurse bustled about, sponging my hot face, bringing clean cool sheets, plumping up pillows.

"This is really sweet of you," I said.

She gave me a startled look, like I'd said something bizarre.

"I seem to have forgotten your name," I said apologetically. "This illness has made me feel a bit confused."

"Dey call mi Quasha," the old woman said. "But mi true name Quashiba. In Africa times, all girls born on a Sunday called dat."

I gasped. "Omigosh, we're in Africa! I had no idea."

She laughed. "Dis not Africa! Dis place Fruitful Vale, your uncle's plantation. You don' remember Massa Bexford and Lovey meet you at di harbour, drive you here to Fruitful Vale?"

I shook my head. "I don't remember a thing. What happened to me?"

"You got sick on the boat, girl-chile," she said. "Missus don' think you gonna live."

Quashiba told me that on my first night, I'd become delirious and wandered out in a hurricane. But my uncle's driver, a man called Lovey, found me before I came to any harm.

This was getting more bewildering every minute. How could I have forgotten who I was?

It made me genuinely panicky. I felt as if I couldn't breathe.

Gotta get some air, I thought urgently. Deep breaths.

"Can you open the shutters?" I asked Quashiba. "It's quite stuffy in here."

There was no glass in the window, just slats you opened or closed. Quashiba pulled a lever, letting in shimmery bars of moonlight. The room filled with the high shrill sounds of crickets. Delicious scents floated in out of the darkness. I lay back on my pillows. The night breeze felt blissful on my sweaty skin. I could see the blue-white pulsing of a star between the wooden slats. And suddenly I knew.

"I'm in Jamaica!" I breathed.

Quashiba clapped her hands. "You remember, eh! You in Jamaica in Fruitful Vale. Your uncle, Massa Josiah Bexford, own all di lan' from here to Orange Park."

I had to turn my face to the wall. Relief at getting my memory back was making me weepy and I didn't want Quashiba to see. I didn't belong in this place. I wasn't even human. I was an undercover angel on a mission to help a friend get back his self-respect. My portal had mysteriously autodestructed on the way. By a miracle, I'd survived unscathed. Apart from a touch of cosmic amnesia.

I burrowed into my pillows. Just as soon as I had my strength back, I'd have to track Brice and Lola down. Hopefully it wasn't too late. Hopefully we could keep our joint date with destiny.

First, I thought, I'll have a tiny little snooze...

Angels have fabulous powers of recovery! Next morning I was tucking into a Jamaican-style breakfast on the veranda outside my room.

I'd just started on the yummy fried plantain, when a white lady with a parasol appeared on the steps. My "Aunt Sarah" had heard of my recovery.

"I am relieved to see you are better, niece." My aunt looked flushed and hot in her tightly-laced gown. I heard her corsets creak as she bent to kiss my cheek. She caught sight of my plate. "What was Quasha thinking!" she exclaimed. "Bringing you this revolting native food!"

"I asked her to. I love yam and plantain," I said in surprise.

Aunt Sarah looked faint. "Oh, but my *dear*, wouldn't you prefer something less *foreign*? A cup of beef tea? Or calves' foot jelly?"

Euw! The foods my aunt thought suitable for invalids sounded far, far more weird than yam!

To my relief my aunt totally accepted that I was the human in my Agency cover story. Though to be quite honest with you, I think Aunt Sarah would have talked to anyone. I shouldn't be mean, but she just about talked my ears off. Apologising about a million times for not nursing me herself, and hinting at a v.

mysterious loss that had left her feeling very low.

"I fear that in my depressed condition I would have caught the contagion and become ill myself," she said.

I didn't like to pry into her personal business but I could tell my aunt was hoping for a reaction, so I said sympathetically, "Omigosh, what happened?"

Aunt Sarah dabbed her eyes with a lace hankie. "Little Phoebe died," she said. "I didn't know it was possible to shed so many tears."

Well, I couldn't just leave it hanging.

"Don't tell me if it upsets you," I said in my gentlest voice. "But who was, erm, Phoebe?"

"My love bird," choked Aunt Sarah. "Every time I see that empty cage..." My aunt quickly turned away, her shoulders shaking.

I felt really sorry for her actually. No one should have to be that lonely, should they?

I thought I'd try to distract her by asking if I could see around the house. I was still in my nightie, but Aunt Sarah caught hold of my hand like a little girl who wants to be best friends, and led me eagerly along dimly lit corridors. She explained that the shutters had to be kept closed to protect her furniture from the strong Jamaican sunlight.

"I had everything sent out from England," she said proudly.

I think Aunt Sarah probably had more English furniture than they had in England. Stiff English chairs upholstered in flowery satin. Huge oil paintings of glowering English ancestors. Highly polished cabinets crammed with English china and glassware that looked totally unused. It wasn't a home at all. It was a museum.

As we walked through this totally depressing series of rooms Aunt Sarah confided how difficult she found life in the tropics. The snakes. The heat. The humidity. "And that terrible hurricane, my dear! I thought the roof was going to blow right off!"

I had an alarming thought. "When was the hurricane exactly?"

"A week ago today. You'd just arrived, poor child, when it started to blow."

*Eep!* I thought. The Agency would be wondering why I hadn't called home. I felt furtively under the collar of my nightdress and went weak with relief. The tags were still there.

"Have you tried sugar cane yet? You really must!" Aunt Sarah smiled properly for the first time and I was horrified to see gruesome black stumps. Sugar cane was obviously one foreign food my aunt enjoyed to the max.

I'd never seen cane growing, so my aunt took me on to a veranda with a view over cane fields. After the permanent twilight inside the house, my eyes were totally dazzled by the acres of lush tropical foliage.

"It's an amazing colour," I breathed. "Almost blue!"

"When cane stalks turn that blue popinjay colour, it means the cane is ripe. My husband starts harvesting when the Christmas breeze begins to blow." She gestured at the palm trees busily clacking their fronds like gossipy grannies.

I was confused. "Is it Christmas then?"

My aunt laughed with a flash of her disturbing teeth. "Everything must seem strange to you, my dear."

"It does seem quite strange," I said truthfully.

Aunt Sarah patted my shoulder. "It will be good to have some female company. The men only come indoors to eat and sleep. And quarrel," she added with a sigh.

"Don't they get on?"

"My nephew, that's your cousin, Beau, and Mr Bexford are constantly at loggerheads. Mr Bexford's brother sent Beau out to Jamaica to learn the plantation business. My husband says he is a foolish young hothead. And Beau says—" My aunt stopped herself abruptly. "Listen to me rattling on! Now you are up and about again, we shall be able to talk every day!"

"Yes, that will be lovely," I said brightly.

I really hope I find the others soon, I thought nervously, as my aunt launched into another long story about her difficult nephew.

You can't afford to let yourself get distracted on a mission, or you'd never get anywhere. I was sorry for my aunt but I hadn't come to Earth to be her full-time companion.

Luckily, Aunt Sarah remembered she had to see the cook about a blancmange or whatever, so I was able to escape. I rushed back to my room, struggled into my seventeenth-century clothes, (with help from Quashiba) and took myself for a walk in the Caribbean sunshine.

Omigosh, how *did* European women survive, wearing that dreadful underwear? I was practically fainting after five minutes. I literally had to rest under a mango tree, like a frail heroine in an old-fashioned book.

It was lovely actually. I could feel calm mango-tree vibes humming inside the tree's knobbly bark. "Hi tree," I whispered. "I'm a visiting angel, but you knew that, didn't you?"

There was no one around, so I took the opportunity to call home. I clasped my angel tags, and tried to tune into my heavenly energy source – and got absolutely *nada*. I couldn't believe it, I'd been here *days* and communications were STILL down!

I could feel myself starting to panic. Don't be a quitter, Melanie, I told myself firmly. The glitch could be just one way. The Agency may still be able to pick up incoming calls.

I beamed a quick progress report to Angel HQ on the off chance that some junior agent would pick up my signal.

*Hi, this is Melanie. Erm, I just wanted you to know I'm fine. I had, erm, a little setback but don't worry, I'm back on the case and hopefully I'll run into the others any time now. Erm later!*

Not the most polished performance, but I'd got distracted halfway through. Beautiful, spine-tingling harmonies came and went on the Caribbean breeze. The cane-cutters were singing.

I gazed across fields, hazy with heat, at the figures working their way steadily down the rows. The rhythm of the singing perfectly fitted the swing-and-slash motion of the workers, as they hacked down the cane.

Something in their voices brought me out in goosebumps. I suddenly felt this intense emotion welling up inside me. The only word to describe it is suffering. A pain and suffering too deep for tears.

These weren't my feelings. I could feel them seeping out of the earth and rocks, and quivering through the mango tree. They were coming from the island itself.

It doesn't make sense, I thought. Jamaica is the closest thing I've seen to Heaven on Planet Earth. What could be wrong with Paradise?

I saw someone strolling towards me through the heat haze and hastily pulled myself together.

There was something oddly familiar about him.

This person had a stiff way of walking, and he wore strange, stiff, seventeenth-century clothes, yet he totally reminded me of— Omigosh, it WAS! It was Brice!!

I rushed to meet him, almost weeping with relief.

"Thank goodness you're safe! I've been SO worried!"

I babbled on about the hurricane and my illness, "I'm SO sorry! I must have set our mission back by *aeons*, but I'm fine now. We can get started any time you say!"

I finally stopped for breath. Brice looked surprisingly dashing in his baggy shirt and knee breeches. Plus he totally had seventeenth-century manners.

"Calm yourself, cousin," he said. "You are not quite recovered, I fear."

"Oooh!" I teased. "That's no way to greet your heavenly rescuer!"

Brice gave me a strange look. "Do I seem as if I need rescuing?"

"Well duh! Obviously you don't! But we didn't know that, since you never actually bothered to phone home! Angel HQ wanted to call off the whole mission, can you believe! But I said to leave you exactly where you are, because you were a big angel now and you'd handle it."

I was grinning like a loon. Brice was not grinning back.

"You should not be walking out of doors at this time of day," he said in a disapproving tone. "You may have a brain fever."

"OK, drop the act, angel boy!" I sighed. "It's getting tedious now. I want to hear the game plan – I assume you guys *do* have a game plan?"

But Brice seemed determined to kid around. "Didn't Aunt Sarah tell you that you must never walk outdoors without your parasol? Particularly in the middle of the day?"

"Oh ha ha! Like I'd be seen dead with a stupid para—"

I broke off. The chilling truth dawned on me.

*Brice wasn't kidding.*

Stay calm babe, I told myself. Better find out how bad this is.

My heart was banging around in my chest, but I managed to fake a ditzy giggle. "Silly me! I can't seem to remember what they call you! My memory is just all over the place."

Brice gave a curt nod. "It is to be expected after such a severe illness. I am your cousin Beau."

Omigosh, I thought. Tell me this isn't happening.

"You've turned pale, little cousin," he said gallantly. "Lean on me if you feel faint."

I felt faint all right. My deluded angel buddy seemed to think he was the human in his Agency story line. What in the world was I going to do?

Beau/Brice had begun to lead me back towards the house.

"*Wait!*" I said desperately. "I absolutely don't have brain fever. I feel fine, truly. And I was just teasing about the angel thing." I faked peals of laughter. "You should have seen your face!"

Brice dropped my arm abruptly. "You have an unusual sense of humour," he said coldly.

I giggled madly. "Everyone says that. But I truly meant no harm. I was just, erm, amusing myself talking nonsense!"

I thought this sounded convincingly seventeenth century, but Brice frowned. "I have no time to talk nonsense to young ladies. My uncle had to stay over at our plantation in

Savannah la Mar. I have to take care of business in his absence. I was on my way to the mill when I saw you."

"Can't I come?" I coaxed. "I've been indoors for days."

"The mill is no place for a young English lady," said Brice stiffly.

I clasped my hands. "Please! I'll just watch. I won't get in the way."

He sighed. "Very well. But fetch your parasol."

"I'll be back in two ticks! Don't move!"

I picked up my skirts and went skipping back to the house, like an innocent little orphan. Inside I was in turmoil.

It absolutely wasn't safe for Brice to be here in this state. An angel with this level of cosmic amnesia was a sitting target for the PODS. I had to get him home. How do you plan to do that, babe? I asked myself. Communications are down or had you forgotten?

We'd managed to get Reuben back to Heaven that time in Elizabethan England, I remembered, but Lola had been with me then. Two angels can send much, much stronger angelic signals than one.

There's your answer, Mel, I thought. Now stop making mountains out of molehills. Together Lola and I can definitely generate enough angel power to get an SOS to Heaven. Sorted!

All I had to do was find her.

# CHAPTER FIVE

"Those are called trumpet trees." Brice pointed to a grove of immensely tall, very slender trees. I'm not sure why they were called trumpet trees. Their leaves looked more like huge fans.

We were walking along a shady track; walking very slowly actually. I know it was hot, but I have to say Beau/Brice didn't seem that keen to reach our uncle's sugar mill. He kept stopping to show me tropical plants along the way.

I dutifully repeated their names to show I was paying attention. Rose apple, soursop, guango trees. All the time I was trying to think of a way to drop Lola casually into the conversation. Asking if he'd run into any nice angels recently was obviously out. I could try asking if he had any other female cousins living nearby? The Agency had made me and Brice relations, so chances were they'd made Lola some kind of rellie too.

If ONLY I'd read my friend's bio...

*Or even your own, babe*, my inner angel commented.

I heard scuffling sounds. A little girl came stumbling down the track in her bare feet, struggling to balance a basket on her head. Her dress was so tattered it was virtually hanging off one shoulder. She lowered her eyes, mumbling, "Morning Massa. Morning miss," as she staggered past.

"Morning, Bright Eyes," Brice called.

The little girl made me think of my little sister Jade. "Bright Eyes is a sweet name," I said wistfully. "And she does have lovely eyes."

"She's very light-skinned, did you notice?" Brice sounded edgy.

"Not really," I said. "People come in all colours, don't they?"

He sighed. "I keep forgetting you've just come from England. In a few months you'll be like all the other white people on this island. It's their curse. They can't escape."

"You're a white person too," I pointed out. "Will you escape?"

He gave a bitter laugh. "I think I was born an outlaw."

Babe, you have no idea, I thought.

A cool whirr of wings fanned my face. A magical little bird appeared in front of us, hovering over a bush of vivid pink blossoms. Its wings were vibrating so fast they were literally a blur. The tiny bird plunged a long, needle-like beak into a blossom, to drink the invisible liquid inside, then whirred away.

"Was that a real humming bird?" I breathed.

"They're as common as blackbirds here. The best time to see them is at sunrise, or just after the rain."

I explained that humming birds were on my personal list of Caribbean "must-sees", along with fireflies.

Brice gave me a sad half-smile. "Do you think you will like Jamaica?"

"It's beautiful," I said. "But I haven't really been here long enough to know if I'll like it."

We were walking past large rhubarb-type plants which Brice said were cocoa plants. They had leaves like heart-shaped umbrellas, easily as big as dinner plates.

"Jamaica is a place you either love or hate!" he said. "I love it, but I hate what we have done to it in a few short years."

"Have you been living here long?" I asked slyly. I was kind of interested to hear what he'd come up with. But it's like he didn't hear.

"Have you heard of the Taino?" Brice asked out of the blue.

"Not really, I don't know much about Jamaica at all." I blushed. "The Taino IS a Jamaican thing, right?"

"Taino means 'good and noble people'. It's what the indigenous Indians of this island called themselves: the people who lived here before the Europeans came."

"I had no idea anyone lived here," I said guiltily.

"There were many such tribes, all with different names, scattered throughout the Caribbean, but white people prefer to forget about them. They like to pretend the New World was empty when Columbus got here. Though they are extremely interested in the cities the original inhabitants are supposed to have left behind."

"These Indians actually built cities?" I'd imagined them living in tepees and whatever.

"They lived simply, in complete harmony with the Earth. But they were also wonderfully skilled craftsmen. For instance, the Taino knew how to use seashells so cleverly that they looked like precious gemstones."

"So what was that you said about a city?"

Brice explained that the first Europeans to arrive in the New World heard tantalising rumours of an ancient city buried deep in a jungle in the Americas. The details varied. Generally the city had been abandoned owing to some horrific natural disaster. In some stories, the city was in Venezuela, sometimes Mexico or Surinam. But the crucial element of the story never changed. There were always fabulous quantities of Indian gold.

Brice gave a painful laugh. "Many white explorers have died attempting to find this city. You could see it as poetic justice."

I sensed that there was something he wasn't telling me. "But what happened to the Taino themselves?"

"Sometimes I think I see their spirits in the woods," he said in a low voice.

The blue sky was cloudless yet I shivered as if a shadow had slipped between us and the sun. "They're *dead*? ALL the Taino?"

"Almost all. A few tribesmen survive in the hills."

"But why would anyone…?"

Brice swallowed. "They got in our way."

After that we just walked on without speaking. But the sound of our shoes rustling through dead and dying leaves suddenly seemed abnormally loud. The idea of ghostly tribesmen watching us from between the trees really disturbed me.

I was becoming aware of an overpowering pong, sickly-sweet and unbelievably foul. Eventually I had to cover my nose.

"You can smell the molasses," Brice explained. "Take my handkerchief."

Shortly afterwards we crossed into the mill yard. This wasn't some picturesque windmill, like mills in picture books. It was powered by six sweating oxen, urged on by drivers with curses and thumps. Instead of mill stones, the sugar mill had three gigantic vertical rollers, as fat as tree trunks and as tall as your average seventeenth-century adult male.

The rollers revolved with hollow rumbling sounds that echoed through the cobbled yard. You could feel it vibrating in your bones and the roots of your teeth. Men were working frantically to keep this monster fed, unloading harvested cane from the carts, stripping away the useless cane trash with knives. The dust and little loose fibres from the trash got everywhere, drifting around our feet, blowing in the workers' eyes.

"The original Taino word for Jamaica was *Xaymaca*," Brice said into my ear. "It means Land of Wood and Water. Wonder what they'd think of it now?"

He was angry. Why wouldn't he be? He was seeing the world through an angel's eyes. As I looked around at this hellish scene, I felt angry too.

The mill workers were all half-naked except for filthy loincloths. Many had ugly scars on their sweating backs and legs. Some had fingers, or parts of fingers, missing. All of them were black.

Brice kept up his grim commentary in my ear, as we made our way through rising clouds of dust.

"Our last mill-feeder, Mingo, got so tired he fell asleep on his feet and lost his hand in the press. He was lucky."

I stared at him. "He was *lucky*?"

"Mingo's brother got dragged in through the rollers last year."

We watched the new mill-feeder deftly handfeeding cane stalks through the rollers, risking his life with every stalk. Treacly brown liquid spurted into a trough at his feet. I tried not to picture Mingo's brother's body being crushed like sugar cane, his red blood mixing with the molasses.

I followed Brice into the boiling house. It was like being inside an oven. I could literally feel the moisture being drawn from my body. The combination of the tremendous heat and molasses fumes, made it next to impossible to breathe.

Five giant copper kettles were suspended over a blazing furnace. Inside the kettles, the boiling molasses blipped and bubbled like an evil magician's brew.

A half-naked boy, of eight or nine years old, was keeping the furnace going with bundles of cane trash. He'd reached the zombie stage of exhaustion, running mechanically from the trash pile to the boiling kettles, from the kettles to the trash pile.

I was fuming by this time. What were the Bexfords *thinking*, making people work in these horrific conditions? Suppose some of that scalding sludge splashed on the little boy's skin? Suppose he stumbled and knocked a kettle flying? The blistering-hot molasses would stick like boiling glue.

Brice had to talk business to the overseer, a sandy-haired Scot and the only white worker in the yard. I grabbed the chance to beam loving vibes to the little boy, then I went outside and beamed heaps more to the mill-feeder. Reuben says it's WAY better to light one tiny candle than to whinge about the dark.

I can't say, obviously, if beaming vibes helped dispel any cosmic darkness for those humans, but it had a huge effect on me.

I found myself taking a hard look at the overseer. When Brice emerged, mopping his perspiring face, my question just burst out.

"Why does that man have a whip?"

An alarmed ripple went round the yard. Brice hurried me out of earshot. "Where have you been hiding, cousin?" he hissed furiously. "Why do you *think* that man has a whip? To show my uncle's slaves who has the power. To stop them rising up and killing their owners in their beds – shall I go on?"

I couldn't speak. At some point I thought I might want to be sick.

"Slaves?" I whispered. "Those people are slaves?"

Brice gave an angry laugh. "Do you imagine plantation owners could live like emperors if we PAID our workers?"

The clues had been there from the start. The pride and pain in Quashiba's voice when she talked about African names. The haunted harmonies floating from the fields, the suffering that came seeping out of the blood-soaked earth of Jamaica itself.

I had no excuse for my ignorance. We had learned all about this particular form of slavery at my old school. Human slavers stole thousands and millions of other humans from Africa, shipping them across the sea to work in the plantations of the Caribbean, and forcing them to work in the conditions I'd just seen.

Yet I'd pushed this information to the back of my mind. I'd wanted to have my own cool little Caribbean experience. Like la la la, hello humming birds, hello mango trees...

STOP IT! I told myself.

Slavery was way too dark to take on by myself. I had to concentrate on my own small cosmic task; getting Brice back home to Heaven before he got into any worse trouble.

To do this, I needed angelic backup, and I didn't want to waste another minute faffing around. I had the definite feeling time was running out.

"I need to find a girl called Lola," I blurted out. "Do you know her? Quashiba says she can sew." I was improvising frantically.

Brice looked totally thunderstruck, then tried to cover his shock. "Erm, yes," he said in a slightly too-casual voice. "I do, indeed, know a Lola."

I was so happy, I almost hugged him!

"*Really!*" I said. I literally felt giddy with relief. This was the best news I'd had since I left Heaven.

You see Mel, I told myself, the simple approach is often the best!

A teeny worm of doubt crept in. "I expect she lives a long way away, doesn't she?"

"If we're talking about the same person, she lives here at Fruitful Vale. But I don't think it can be the same Lola." Brice sounded really cagey but this clue passed me by.

"No, it is. It has to be," I burbled. "Can you take me to her?"

"I don't think I can, no," he said, to my dismay. "Anyway, I don't think Lola would want visitors."

"Why ever not?"

He couldn't meet my eyes. "Before you arrived from England, Lola was accused of stealing from the kitchen. My uncle has strong opinions about stealing. The overseer gave her a beating."

I gave a nervous laugh. "No, no, sorry, we're getting our wires crossed. This Lola's an – a – very proud person." I was so freaked that I'd almost said "angel"! "She doesn't steal from kitchens," I added firmly.

Brice swallowed. "To my uncle she is just another thieving slave."

There was a sudden humming in my ears. The dusty mill yard, with its feverish activity, wobbled like a mirage.

"She *can't* be a slave!" I whispered. "Lola's not even African!"

I immediately wanted to bite my tongue off. What a dumb thing to say. Like, if she'd been pure African it would be OK to beat her like a dog.

Brice gave his painful laugh. "One drop of African blood is enough to condemn someone to a life of slavery. I heard an entertaining debate between my uncle and an English vicar who'd recently arrived in Jamaica. They were trying to decide whether Africans have souls. I suggested it would be more educational to find out whether plantation owners have souls."

"I have to see her," I told him shakily. "It's vitally important!" Horror was pulsing through me in waves. While I'd been lolling around convalescing, my friend had been suffering the worst humiliation Planet Earth had to offer.

Brice sounded despairing. "Lola was sold a few days ago."

My heart almost stopped with fright. "She's GONE! But you said—"

"I meant there's no point you going to see her. Lovey is driving her over to St Mary's first thing tomorrow."

I'd only just got here in time.

I caught hold of his sleeve. "Take me to her. Take me now!" I must have sounded mad.

"I can't. My uncle could come back at any moment. He would be extremely displeased if—"

"I don't CARE!"

Bruce looked suspicious. "Forgive me, but what exactly is so important about this piece of sewing?" Brice asked.

I grabbed at the first excuse that came into my head. "I, erm, lost heaps of weight while I was ill. I've got this gorgeous dress for the Christmas party and now it totally won't fit. I need Lola to alter it before she goes."

Brice looked disgusted and no wonder. He must have thought I was turning into one of those ugly Europeans before his eyes. But he nodded reluctantly. "Very well."

The slave huts had been built as far as possible from the main house, behind a natural screen of coconut palms. The huts were thatched with palm leaves, and looked and smelled completely squalid. Garbage lay rotting everywhere. I suppose no one had the heart to clean up.

There was unexpected beauty though, even in this depressing little village. The garden plots where slaves grew their own fruits and vegetables glowed with life and colour. I could literally feel the love and care that went into them.

An old man crouched outside his hut, tying up a flowering vine that had come away from its stake. "Massa," he mumbled.

His eyes followed us resentfully as we walked past. I could feel other pairs of eyes watching from the dark, strong-smelling interiors of the huts. The hostility in the air made it hard to breathe.

I hoped Brice was wrong. I hoped the ghosts of the Taino weren't watching what Europeans were doing to their peaceful Land of Wood and Water. In just two hundred years, it had been turned into a hellhole.

I was finding Jamaica's dark side way too hard to handle. But I told myself I didn't have to handle it much longer.

Once I'd hooked up with Lola, we'd all be zooming back home.

I tried to make my voice sound casual. "Which hut is Lola's?"

Brice pointed. "Hurry. My uncle could come back any minute."

The path to Lola's hut was edged with rough scented grasses. I tore off a blade as I passed, inhaling its lemony perfume. I was nervous for no reason. Lola's on your side, fool, I reminded myself. Pretty soon this will all be over. This time tomorrow lover boy will have his memory back and we'll all be drinking hot chocolate at Guru.

The door to Lola's hut was open. Inside was a woven sleeping mat and an old cast-iron cooking pot. Balanced over the stewpot was a crudely shaped wooden spoon, carved out of some kind of gourd. It seemed that these three pitiful objects were the sum total of her possessions.

I remembered Brice arguing furiously with Mr Allbright about a week after he joined our history class. "Millions of human children are dying of hunger because rich countries couldn't care if they live or die! And the powers that be say we mustn't interfere with their free will! Well, that sucks! If you want humans to change, angels are going to have to make waves!"

I stared at that dented old stewpot and I wanted to make waves, like you would not believe. I wanted a humungous tidal wave to roll in and wash slavery from the face of the Earth for ever.

I was feeling electricky tingles, normally a sure sign that other celestial agents are in the area. The thought of seeing Lola was such a relief, I practically fell over myself to get to the rear of her hut.

A golden-skinned girl in a fraying head-tie was stretching up to peg a tattered cotton blouse on the line. She winced and clutched her side.

I ran forward. "Lola? Are you OK?"

She spun in terror then clutched her chest. "Miss! You frighten mi. Mi tink a bad duppy creep up when mi nah lookin'."

I felt confused. This girl looked like Lola, but she didn't sound or act like her.

Don't be stupid, Mel, who else could she be? I told myself quickly.

Yet something was off. Lollie and I normally hug, even if we've only been apart for like, *a day*. But I got the definite feeling that hugging would not be a wise move. My friend was keeping her eyes fixed stonily on the ground, as if she didn't want me to know what she was thinking.

That was another disturbing thing. Lola and I almost always do know what each other is thinking. Now she was completely shut down. I could just feel incredibly hostile vibes.

She's angry, I thought shakily. She thinks I abandoned her.

I swallowed. "You've had a terrible time," I said. "Did the overseer really beat you?"

"Mi belong Massa," Lola said in a sullen voice. "Massa can do what him like."

The soles of her bare feet were filthy from walking about the plantation without any shoes. She was wearing a shapeless old skirt and blouse in faded blue. The same sun-faded blue cotton I'd seen on Quashiba and Bright Eyes. Slave clothes.

I felt my heart contract. "Lollie, I swear, I've been ill, or I'd have come sooner."

"Mi hear 'bout dat," she said in her new singsong voice. "Lovey find you in di bush. Dey say you like to die."

My best friend sounded like she wouldn't have cared either way.

"Babe, drop the slave-talk, please!" I pleaded. "This isn't you."

Lola made a rude sound, like sucking spit through her teeth. "Nuttin wrong wid me, miss. You di one talkin' foolishness."

"Lola, LOOK at me!" I practically yelled at her.

My friend reluctantly met my eyes, and I felt as if I was falling through space. There was no warmth, no spark of recognition. Just pure hate.

"You really don't know who I am," I whispered.

Beau/Brice came up behind us, looking frazzled.

"I see you're up and about, Lola," he said in a falsely bright voice. "The pain isn't too bad today?"

Lola blushed. "No, Massa," she said. "Pain nah so bad today."

The two of them were being just a bit too careful not to look at each other. Brice and Lola might have lost their memories but they definitely hadn't lost their cosmic chemistry.

Their obvious attraction only made me feel worse.

I felt so alone, I can't tell you. I wanted to wake up in my room at school, and rush next door to Lola. I wanted to tell her about the horrible dream I just had where we were on a nightmare mission to Jamaica, but she'd somehow forgotten we were friends. I wanted to hear her say, "Poor you, babe! Dreams are SO weird!"

But my nightmare still went on. I turned and fled back to the house.

My aunt was sitting on her veranda, chewing furiously on a chunk of sugar cane. Beside her was a dish of mangled spat-out stalks. As I fled past, she called brightly, "Would you like to sample some, my dear! Sugar cane is so soothing to the nerves."

I looked at this woman who wept over dead birds while her husband tortured human slaves, and I wanted to despise her, but I knew she was as lonely and lost as her slaves.

I excused myself, saying I needed to rest. Then I shut myself in my room and threw myself on my bed. I was so upset I couldn't even cry. What am I going to do? I thought. What am I going to DO?

Somewhere between Heaven and Earth, something had happened to my friends; something which made them forget their true identities. Unlike yours truly, Lola and Brice had clearly read their cover stories. Now they believed they actually were these fictional humans. They were living their parts for real.

This mission was meant to get Brice back on his feet. Instead he and Lola had been ensnared in some dark game of seventeenth-century Consequences. *White nephew of rich plantation owner meets fiesty slave-girl in steamy Jamaica. And the consequence was...*

I was playing a lonely game of angels all by myself.

I truly don't think I have ever felt so alone. I won't lie to you, I could feel myself being sucked down into this like, total *marsh* of self-pity.

But then I did something that I think shows I'm starting to mature as a celestial trainee: I asked my inner angel for advice.

I sat down in the lotus position and closed my eyes. After a while I felt the familiar burning hot-potato sensation spreading through my chest. I don't see my inner angel. It's more like I could feel her vibes building up inside me. And this time I heard her voice as clear as a bell.

"Hi babe," Helix said. "Poor you! It must be scary, seeing your friends like this."

My eyes filled with tears. "It's so scary I can't tell you. It's like they've been hypnotised."

"Isn't it?" she agreed warmly. "Lola isn't a slave.

Brice isn't her master's nephew. It's just a story line some Agency scriptwriter thought up for them.

"I'm so confused, Helix. How come this kind of thing can happen to angels?"

"It's a bummer," she said. "The fact is, thoughts are incredibly powerful. On Earth, if you think something's true, it usually becomes true."

"For humans, yeah," I objected. "But we're supposed to know how this stuff works!"

"OK, OK, listen. Angels are immortal beings operating at v. intense energy levels, right?"

"Right," I agreed.

"Plus they have humungous thought power, agreed?"

I remembered how the angel preschoolers grew teeny baby trees in like, ten minutes flat. "Agreed," I said.

"Without their angel memories, Brice and Lola grabbed at what seemed to be reality. They're actually creating this whole scenario minute by minute. If they saw what was happening, they could step out into angelic reality just like that. But to them it feels like this *is* reality."

"Actually it kind of feels like reality to me too," I said miserably.

"I know, hon. So here's a teeny cosmic hint. If something makes you feel small, lost and hopeless, it probably isn't real!!"

Helix went on to tell me some other private angelic stuff, which I'm not supposed to share. After what seemed like blissful aeons of time, I opened my eyes.

It was amazing! I had bags of energy suddenly. All my self-pity had vanished, and I saw the whole thing with total clarity. And I knew now why I'd had to come on Brice's mission.

It was like that gruesome fairy story about the three blind old women, who had to share one eye between them.

I had to see for all of us. And I had to remember for all of us. But I couldn't do that if I got sucked into the illusion along with my friends. It seemed like Brice, Lola and I were trapped in separate movies. It even seemed like my soul-mate hated me. But these were just illusions.

Lola and I had a truly special bond. Even before we met, we were already connected. This connection was still there, even if Lola couldn't see or feel it. I just had to find a way to remind her. I had to find a way to help my best friend see through her fog of cosmic amnesia. I'd creep out after dark and go to her hut. Whatever it took to get through to Lola, I'd do.

Now that I had a plan, it seemed OK to have a little siesta.

When I woke up it was dark. I smoothed down my crumpled gown, put on my seventeenth-century cotton cap and little leather slippers and crept out of the house.

Stars sparkled high above the plantation. Some of the stars were so tiny they were just scatters of glitter dust. Crickets sang their metallic 'sweet-sweet' song from every tree and bush, like a chorus of tiny bicycle bells. And I became aware of another faint, thrilling sound vibrating through the night like a heartbeat. A faraway beating of drums.

As I got nearer to the slave quarters, I saw the flicker of cooking fires through the palms. I could hear voices murmuring, sounding warm and intimate in the dark. I felt all the fine hairs rise on the back of my neck. The Bexfords had a piece of Africa, right here in their back yard; a living, breathing, stolen piece of Africa. A three-year-old child would know how precious this was. Yet the Bexfords and their kind had no idea.

I had to pinch myself. "You're in Jamaica, Melanie..." I whispered. "You're in Jamaica, listening to African slaves talking in the dark."

I can't explain why, exactly, but I felt like I was supposed to be here. I felt, I don't know, *honoured*. I glanced up at the stars, and for a moment I had a dizzy sense of being part of that vast shimmery totally mysterious pattern.

I must have been invisible standing in the shadowy coconut grove, because two figures sped softly past me without even noticing I was there. It was Brice and Lola! "What on earth?" I gasped.

I raced after them, trying not to trip over my stupid gown, and finally caught them up in the stables.

A lighted lantern made a pool of weak yellowish light. A horse was nervously shifting its hooves on the straw. I saw the whites of its eyes gleaming. Brice was murmuring soothing words as he adjusted the saddle.

"What's going on?" I said breathlessly.

My friends froze guiltily. I could see Lola's pulse beating in her throat. I could smell hay and horses, and the strong-smelling coconut oil she used on her hair.

"Mi tell you dat white girl bring trouble!" she hissed to Brice as if I wasn't there. "She tell Ole Massa for sure!"

"Who am I? The secret police?" I said angrily. "Don't be stupid. I'm not going to tell anyone."

It might be an illusion, but Lola's hostility was really hard to take.

Brice fastened the girth on the nervous horse. "We're leaving this place."

"I'd sort of worked that out," I said. "Where are you running to?"

"Don' tell her, Massa!" Lola cried. "Ole Massa set dogs on wi."

I took several deep breaths. "I'm not your enemy. I won't tell. You don't have to be scared of me, OK?"

The sound of drumming was getting louder, as if the wind had suddenly changed. A horse whickered from its stall.

Lola shot me a look, half scared, half triumphant. "Mi nah scared a you!" she said. "Young Massa buy wi freedom. He buy all wi freedom!"

I was stunned. "He's going to free you ALL?"

"Just our slaves at first," Brice explained. "There's a place up in the hills. People call it

Cockpit country. Hundreds of runaway slaves live up there."

Isn't that incredible. Brice couldn't remember his name or heavenly address. He certainly had no memory of the Agency. Yet he had made up his mind to save slaves single-handed. It's like he *knew* he was supposed to be on a mission. He'd just forgotten he didn't have to do it alone.

If this had been the normal Brice I could have reasoned with him. I could have said, "You tried that rescue-trip before and it got you into deep poo." Brice's previous rescue attempt ended in a long and gruesome exile in the Hell dimensions, where he only survived by doing freelance work for a number of Dark agencies.

But the Beau Bexford Brice didn't know about Hell dimensions or warring cosmic agencies. He was saving the world, the only way he knew how. So I stuck to basics. "Where are you going to get that kind of money?"

"You don't need to worry about that," he said cagily.

Please, please say he isn't planning a robbery, I prayed. I didn't think the Agency would be too thrilled if Brice robbed a bank, even if his motives were *really* pristine. For once I didn't have to think about what to do next.

"I want to go with you!" I said in a bright voice. "I think what you're both doing is, erm, amazing and I want to help."

Lola did her rude tooth-sucking sound. "It look like three people can sit on dat poor lickle horse to you?"

"Then steal two horses, girlfriend," I said. "I'm coming and that's final."

Brice shook his head. "I can't let you do that. I couldn't guarantee your safety."

"I don't care," I said stubbornly. "I'm coming."

Lola was scowling horribly. No way did she want me on their romantic trip! "Tie her to a coconut tree! Massa nah find her till mawnin'."

Illusion or not, Lola's attitude was really getting under my skin. I flashed my sweetest smile. "You tie me up, babe, and I'll scream the place down, and you'll have that whole slavering-hunting-dogs scenario you're anxious to avoid."

Well, I wasn't trying to win a popularity contest. I was following the first law of angelic teamwork. Keep your team together at ALL times.

You need me, I told them silently. I'm your seeing-eye angel.

Perhaps my cosmic vibes got through to him, because Brice reluctantly saddled a second horse. Lola was visibly fuming. Instead of riding with the handsome Young Massa, she was stuck with me.

"Where are we going by the way?" I asked her as we spurred our horses into the night.

Lola's answer gave me the chills.

"Port Royal," she snarled. "Di wickedest city on Earth!"

## CHAPTER SIX

Early next morning, we were riding single file through a misty river gorge. Ladders of sunlight slanted down through the mist. Now and then I had to push aside lush tangles of vines that hung down like curtains. A bird called the same two-note song over and over. It felt like we were all alone at the green dawn of the world.

Well, if it wasn't for the vibes. I'm serious! It's a miracle I didn't break out in blisters! As the morning went on, I genuinely started to wonder if my best friend was plotting to poison me. Lola kept stopping to pick stinky plants she spotted by the track.

"Dis herb good for mi skin, Massa," she'd tell Brice, stuffing some obscene hairy root in her bag. And she'd shoot him this intimate smile. Sometimes she'd tell him it was a herb that would make her hair shine, or whiten her teeth, the scheming little minx. When Brice wasn't looking, she'd dart spiteful looks at me. Like: "You better not cross me, girl, or I'll put these little babies in your stew!"

I was relieved when Brice said we were breaking our journey in a place called Spanish Town. It was getting hot, plus my angelic backside was SO sore. This wasn't really so surprising. My previous horse-riding experience was basically nil.

In Spanish Town a huge street market was in full swing. Old ladies in vividly-coloured head-ties squatted in the shade beside heaps of yams, bananas and sweet potatoes, pots, pans and bales of cloth, singing out to passers-by.

This was the first real town I'd seen since I'd arrived. A little girl ran alongside trying to sell us some freshly-picked oranges. Brice threw her some coins and we rode along, slurping at the greenish-skinned fruit.

"Why's this called Spanish Town?" I asked in a juicy voice.

"The English captured Jamaica from the Spanish," Brice explained. "It's the perfect base for attacking foreign ships."

I was shocked. "Isn't that piracy?"

He grinned. "Piracy is exactly what it is."

"Sorry, I don't believe you," I said primly. "I can't believe the government would encourage pirates."

He laughed out loud. "Why not? The government gets the loot!"

I could feel Lola fidgeting sulkily behind me. I was always trying to include her, but she totally refused to join any conversation I was a part of. The bottom line was: I wasn't meant to be there.

We stopped at an inn on the outskirts and seated ourselves at an outdoor table in the leafy shade of a passion-fruit vine. A slave-girl brought us our breakfast. She looked genuinely shocked to see two white people sitting at the same table as their slave.

Brice and Lola spent the meal whispering to each other. I didn't want to be a gooseberry, so I concentrated on trying to find something I could eat. It was a somewhat weird breakfast, I have to say. The stewed goat looked really stringy, plus there was this evil Jamaican green vegetable that someone had boiled to a slimy pulp. The coconut cake seemed the safest bet. Dry but quite edible, washed down with a beaker of fresh cane juice.

While we ate, a vulture circled lazily overhead in a cloudless blue sky.

Lola shook her fist. "G'way!" she threatened. "You nah get dinner today, John Crow!"

How did Lola KNOW this stuff? I wondered.

My friend had lived in seventeenth-century Jamaica for less than ten days. But when she hummed to herself, she sang authentic slave tunes! She knew which local plants made your hair shiny. She even knew how to tie a head-tie, African-style. And Brice knew all about sugar mills and pirates and stealing horses. It's like my friends had plugged into some cosmic equivalent of the Discovery Channel!

I was still puzzling over this when Brice went off to get supplies. The minute he was out of sight, Lola let me have it.

My Lola has a real way with words. But this Lola came out with stuff that made your eyes water. Even when she was insulting you she talked sheer poetry. Lola told me that young Massa Bexford might be taken in by my sweet innocent manner but she'd had me totally figured from day one.

According to her, I was a little gold-digger determined to get my hooks into my rich cousin. I know! She was convinced I wanted to marry him for his inheritance! According to Lola, also, I was just pretending to care about slaves. White people were all the same, purely out for themselves.

Let me tell you the really disturbing thing. By the time Lola had finished with me I'd started to think she was right. Being white was starting to seem like a really unpleasant disease. I literally felt like I might be emanating a pale poisonous glow. Purely by walking round inside my skin, I was a living advertisement for Evil.

If I'd been human, I think I'd have crawled into some dark hole and died of shame. Lola was meant to be my best friend but she couldn't even see me. It totally broke my heart that Lola couldn't see the real me hurting inside.

I know! It's embarrassing. She's the slave, yet I want *her* to pity me, the poor misunderstood white girl!

I had to shut my eyes to stop the tears from falling.

My inner angel had just been waiting for the chance to put a stop to all this nonsense. A message flashed up on my mental screen: *A soul-mate's colours shine through no matter what.* Lola's parting words.

I felt all the stress drain out through the soles of my feet. Lola wasn't a slave. I was not an evil white-skinned devil. None of this was real. We're just angels, I thought. Angels passing through.

I was so relieved to be back in angelic reality that I was smiling through my tears.

Lola gave a scornful snort. "You laugh like stupid! But you don' know nuttin! You don' even know why we goin' to Port Royal. But Massa tell me. Massa tell mi everyting!"

Poor girl. She was so desperate to prove that the young Massa loved her best that she blurted out the whole plan.

It was complete madness. The whole enterprise depended on Brice selling a treasure map he'd acquired from a pirate called Bermuda Jack, in return for a bottle of rum. This wasn't your regular treasure map, mind you. It was a map leading to an ancient Indian city. A city made of pure gold. I *know*! You couldn't make it up!!

"Massa get a heap a gold for dis map," Lola said proudly. "A whole heap a gold."

"Why are we talking about gold?" Brice had come up behind her.

Lola almost wet herself with shock. She backed away from him, guiltily. "Mi nah want to tell her, Massa. She drag it outa me!"

It's OK, I didn't take it personally. Now I was back in angel mode, I understood exactly where she was coming from. Reuben and I were slaves once in ancient Rome, but unlike Lola, we knew we were undercover angels. If things had been different, who knows how we'd have behaved?

"I'm not angry," Brice consoled her. "I was planning to tell my cousin everything anyway."

And once we were back on the road to Port Royal, my angel buddy told me the whole crazy story.

Brice hadn't bought a map from a pirate. He'd bought HALF a map. Obviously that made me feel much better.

Bermuda Jack had told Brice that if he reached Port Royal before the Christmas breeze stopped blowing, he'd find the owner of the map's missing half staying at a certain tavern in Port Royal. "Jack said she'd give me hundreds of Spanish doubloons for my half," he said eagerly.

"The other owner is a lady?" I said in surprise.

Brice grinned. "A very beautiful lady, by all accounts."

Lola made a noise that sounded exactly like ripping velcro.

"And is the Christmas breeze still blowing?"

He gestured at the palm trees busily clicking their fronds. "It'll blow for a few days yet."

"I hate to be dense," I said. "But why didn't Jack sell his half of the map and pocket the doubloons."

"Oh, he says it's cursed. But that's just superstition," Brice said casually.

See what I mean about that boy? Just as I'm thinking things can't get much crazier, he throws in a curse!

"Naturally, the Taino wanted to discourage Europeans from plundering their sacred golden city," he explained, "so they spread all these stories to warn them off."

"Wait – slow down! This city is SACRED?"

Brice looked shifty. "Allegedly."

"Personally I'm wondering if this Indian city even existed," I said. "Maybe the Taino were just having a laugh?"

"My map is genuine," Brice said confidently.

"But how can you be sure?"

He pulled a crackly piece of parchment out of his shirt. The map fragment was badly scorched at the edges as if it had been rescued from a fire in the nick of time. And the sinister spattering of faded brownish splodges was almost certainly a trail of human bloodstains.

But at the top in shaky script was a name that set my heart racing.

*Coyaba, City of the Gods.*

I'd never heard of this city before, yet when I saw the name, about a zillion angel volts went off inside my head and, like Brice, I knew this was the real thing.

But that just made it worse. I had the definite feeling that Heaven's favourite bad boy was getting in way over his head.

Someone had to make him see sense before he did something we'd all regret. Someone like me.

"Erm, hate to be a party pooper, but if this map is for real, it's incredibly precious. What if this lady in Port Royal is just like all those other Europeans, purely out for herself. Don't you think it's a bit dodgy giving her directions to an ancient golden city? Do you really think the Taino would want her to have their gold?"

Lola gave me a poisonous look. "Massa don' business wid dead people gold," she flashed. "Massa just wan' set wi free."

"But it doesn't belong to him, Lola! Hello! The *City of the Gods*?! Trust me, if you let pirates loose on a sacred Taino city, that could have really dark consequences!"

Brice was glaring at me now. "Slavery also has dark consequences. The Taino are dead. I'm more concerned with the sufferings of the living."

Lola gave me a triumphant smile.

I probably should have left it, but something niggled at the edges of my mind.

"I don't totally understand what you need all these doubloons for," I said to Brice. "Why do you need so much cash?"

"Guns and ammunition are expensive," he said coolly.

My jaw dropped. "Guns and—"

"The rebel slaves deserve all the help we can give, don't you think?"

No need to check Agency policy on this one. I opened my mouth twice, then shut it for good. I didn't feel up to explaining to Brice why this was such a bad idea.

We rode on to Port Royal in a rather strained silence. I tried reminding myself that I was an angel on a mission, but I felt more like a tin can that had accidentally got attached to a v. hyperactive dog. I was supposed to be working on a brilliant strategy to get my friends back to Heaven. Instead I was being dragged helplessly from one insanely complicated situation to the next.

We trotted along the bumpy potholed road, under palm trees waving graceful fronds in the tropical breeze. The sun was hot. The sky was blue. But my heart felt as heavy as lead. I don't know how far it was to Port Royal, but it felt like a long way in that atmosphere, believe me. Gradually the lush vegetation of inland Jamaica was replaced with dry-looking scrub and cacti. By late afternoon I smelled salt on the breeze. Minutes later we rode into a little settlement known as Passage Fort, where we were to get the ferry to Port Royal.

We had to leave the horses at the town's one tavern.

"No horses, mules or horse-drawn carriages are allowed in Port Royal," Brice told us. "The city is barely half a mile wide and extremely densely populated. You will notice the buildings are unusually tall. The city folk soon ran out of building land, and since they couldn't build outwards, they built upwards instead!"

We hurried down to the harbour just as the sun was starting to set. Besides us, there were two other passengers, a nervous white merchant and his very handsome young slave. The slave was hopefully checking Lola out, but she only had eyes for the young Massa.

I really enjoyed that boat trip actually. We passed tiny uninhabited islands looking exactly like tropical islands you see in cartoons.

We were halfway to Port Royal when we heard an appalling ruckus floating across the water. Pistols firing, bells ringing, drunken voices singing and squabbling in every language under the sun, drums beating, whistles blowing. I thought some mad carnival was going on, but Brice said this was normal for Port Royal. With a flash of fear I remembered that Lola had called it the "wickedest city on Earth".

The dock was unbelievably crowded. The moment we got off the boat there was this total stampede. Rough humans of both sexes rushed at us, yelling threateningly in our faces, poking and prodding at us, mostly trying to sell us stuff we didn't want.

This was a city where pirates basically ruled. Its lanes and alleyways swarmed with buccaneers of all colours and nationalities. It even *smelled* wicked. The streets literally stank like they'd been marinaded in Jamaican rum! Just about every other building was a pirate tavern, a gambling den, or a "punch-house". Lola looked disturbed when she saw the punch-house girls with their plunging bodices and crudely made-up faces.

In a street behind the Turtle Market, we passed a gun shop, where pistols were laid out on black velvet like a lady's jewels. A drunken pirate suddenly pushed his face into mine, making kissing noises. He was quite old and his leathery face was seamed with scars.

Lola flew between us and gave him a massive thump in the chest.

"G'way, you boldface devil, you!" she said fiercely. "You tink dis nice girl business wid you! Tcha!"

He slunk away mumbling apologies.

"Thanks, Lola," I said gratefully.

Lola just gave me one of her looks. Like, "You think I *want* to be your babysitter?"

"Do try to look as if you know where you're going," Brice sighed.

On the other side of the street, a pirate dressed in silks and velvets, was stopping passers-by at gunpoint, challenging them to a drinking contest from a barrel of Jamaican rum!

I scurried after Lola and Brice. "And do we? Know where we're going?" I asked nervously.

Brice said we were looking for a tavern called Diego's Whiskers. Naturally, I thought he was kidding. But Brice assured me the name was for real; Diego had been a notorious Spanish pirate who finally got blown to pieces by English buccaneers.

"What was so special about Diego's whiskers?" I asked. "Did they glow in the dark or something?"

Brice grinned. "English seamen are always boasting about singeing their enemies' facial hair," he said. "It's the ultimate insult!"

He seemed more like the old Brice now we'd left the plantation. He seemed thrilled with himself, to be honest: setting off to do a nefarious deal with a mysterious lady, a bloodstained treasure map in his pocket, and an adoring slave-girl by his side.

However, I was getting twitchy. I reckoned it would be dark in about five minutes max. We're talking Jamaican darkness, right? Five short minutes before the streets of dilapidated high-rise tenements turned into inky black canyons. This thought seemed to occur to my friends at approximately the same moment. No one actually mentioned lurking robbers or cut-throats but everyone suddenly picked up the pace.

Brice led us down an extremely evil-smelling alley, running parallel to the waterfront. I could hear the hollow sloshing of waves against wooden piers and the rhythmic creaking of ships' timbers.

We hurried along, scattering pigs and chickens in our haste to get under a roof before nightfall. Brice peered at an inn sign in the gathering dusk. It was peppered with bullet holes and totally impossible to read, but he strode through the door of the tavern without a second's hesitation. Amnesia or no amnesia, the bad-boy radar was functioning as well as ever!

Brice glanced around the crowded bar, nodded matily at the landlord and, without breaking stride, ducked through a door marked PRIVATE.

Lola and I beetled after him, not wanting to be left alone with the pervy old sea dogs who formed Diego's select clientele.

We found ourselves in a long, low room with dark wooden beams. The air was thick with rum and tobacco fumes. A dozen ferocious seafaring-types were yelling at each other through the fog. They'd obviously been drinking heavily for hours, if not days. Every person in this room had an opinion and every person was bellowing his opinion at the top of his lungs, backing it up by hammering his fist or the barrel of his pistol on the table.

But the most opinionated person in that room was actually a girl. A booze-swilling, pistol-toting girl, it's true. But still a girl, no more than sixteen years old.

She had her back to me, so I couldn't tell if she was really beautiful, like people said, but it was obvious she had great style. Her rustling skirts of crimson silk were looped up to reveal creamy lace petticoats and boots of gorgeous Spanish leather. Her shiny black hair had been oiled like a flamenco dancer's and swept up with combs. Rubies and sapphires twinkled on the pirate girl's fingers and swung sparkling from her ears.

Brice coughed. "Sirs, madam?" he said politely. "May I enquire – if this is the right place?"

Ten pirates' hands drew ten swords with a thrilling clash of steel. The eleventh pirate snatched up a chair, aiming it menacingly at Brice's head. He was growling, literally growling like a dog.

The girl started to laugh, a wild tipsy laugh. "You've come to the right place, sir – for a fight!"

She swung to face us, still laughing.

My heart almost stopped. I *knew* this girl!

"Cat!" I breathed. "Cat Darcy?"

I knew this was impossible. Shakespeare's girlfriend would have to be over a hundred and twenty years old by now!

"I am Mariah Darcy," the pirate girl said haughtily. "Catherine Darcy was my grandmother. Who are you, miss? And why do you burst in on our private soiree?"

Brice stepped forward. "I have something in my possession that I was told would interest you."

Mariah gave one of her wild laughs. "Oho! You've been speaking to Bermuda Jack!" She gestured imperiously to her men. "Sheathe your swords! Caleb, stop that ridiculous growling, put down the chair and tell the landlord to bring more rum! These people are our guests."

I was still reeling from the bizarre cosmic coincidence. I could NOT believe we'd bumped into Cat's granddaughter!

She could almost be Cat's double, I thought wonderingly.

Angels aren't meant to get involved with their humans, but on our mission to Elizabethan England, Lola and I developed a genuine affection for Cat Darcy. It was a relief to know she'd eventually found love and had a family. No guy could have measured up to Will Shakespeare obviously. But she'd survived their break-up and made a new life for herself and that was really good news.

But as I gazed at Cat's seventeenth-century descendant, I started to wonder if I was seeing things. I was picking up tiny lightning flashes every time Mariah laughed. Lola seemed equally baffled.

Finally I caught on. At one stage in her pirate career Mariah had lost an eyetooth, and a diamond had been wired into the gap.

Coo-er, I thought. The piracy bizz must be paying really well.

I thought Cat's pirate dad would probably be really proud if he could see his stylish great-granddaughter carrying on the family tradition.

These are the kinds of moments I usually share with Lola, and I instinctively turned to smile at her, but she just blanked me and turned away.

I bravely pulled myself together. One day we'll laugh at this, babe, I told my friend silently. And that's a promise.

It was past three in the morning and the candles at Diego's had almost burned down to tiny stumps.

The remains of a huge pirate feast were scattered over the table. Oyster shells, gnawed pork ribs, the heads of giant prawns. But the drinking went on and on. And Beau Bexford and Mariah found more and more in common.

"Each of us is a freedom fighter in our different ways! Freedom is the most important thing in life, don't you agree?" The pirate girl had been licking pork grease from her fingers, but she stopped to give Brice an intimate smile.

Brice threw down a shot of rum and yelled, "To freedom!"

Mariah let out a wild yodel. "Aye! To freedom!"

Those pirates who could still stand, jumped to their feet and knocked back more slugs of fiery white rum. "To freedom!" they roared.

The pirate girl sat back down, showing lacy petticoats. "Only the souls of outlaws are truly free," she announced. "That's why the world hates us! Isn't that true, men?"

And the other pirates cheered and pounded their fists on the table until the wooden planks vibrated like a drum.

I don't know why, but while you were with Mariah Darcy, you forgot to ask really obvious questions. Like, are you sure that's why people hate you? Are you sure it isn't because you hack off their limbs with cutlasses? Plus the robbing and pillaging might put people off!

It sounds ridiculous, I know, but that night not a word of criticism entered my head. To be honest with you, I admired Mariah to the point of total and utter envy. She had it all. Beauty, brains, her own ship. Plus a loyal band of followers to do her bidding. (No, really! Some of them were quite cute in an unwashed Hell's Angels kind of way!)

At a time when a girl's career options often consisted of being locked away in a convent, or dying hideously in childbirth, this girl had the entire Caribbean ocean for her playground.

What I envied most of all was Mariah Darcy's confidence. You just knew she didn't stay awake at nights, beating herself up over some stupid little mistake. Mariah answered to no one but herself.

And as the night went on, the pirate girl revealed a softer side. OK, so she was a bit woozy from the rum, but she seemed genuinely inspired by Brice's desire to help his father's slaves. She fished her half of the map out of her blouse, and she and Brice placed their two halves side by side so you could see how exactly they fitted.

"Let me tell you something," she slurred. "I could retire from piracy tomorrow, if it was gold I craved."

My buddy's eyes glinted. "Isn't it?"

She shook her head. "I have pots of gold," she boasted. "Crates and barrels full of gold. Gold means nothing to me. What I crave, Mr Bexford, is adventure!"

"Oh really," he said politely. "I thought it was freedom."

She wagged her finger. "Now now, sir! Let's not quibble over words! My point is, like you, I detest all forms of slavery. That's why I'm declining your offer! I've decided NOT to buy your half of the map."

Brice looked confused. "I see. Naturally it's yours to do—"

"I haven't finished, Mr Bexford! I propose, sir, that you and I mount a joint expedition to find this city. Any gold we find will be used to resettle your unhappy slaves." Mariah leaned forward. "What do you say?"

Omigosh how thrilling, I thought excitedly. Say yes!

I know! I was totally caught up in the moment. One night with pirates and my angelic scruples go right out the window!

Brice would have made a great poker player. I could NOT have told you what that boy was thinking. We were all holding our breath, except for Lola, who seemed to be struggling to stay awake.

"What is your answer, Mr Bexford?" Mariah's voice had a bit of an edge this time.

Brice pushed back his chair so dramatically that I truly thought he was going to storm out. "I say we drink another toast," he said coolly. "I accept your generous proposal, Miss Darcy."

Mariah let out a piercing yodel of triumph. The pirates whistled and stomped their feet to show their approval. One of the pirates produced a fiddle and started to play a sea shanty. Another pirate picked up some silver spoons and beat out a lively rhythm.

Brice bowed to Mariah. She took his hand, laughing her tipsy laugh, and they swung each other recklessly around the room as the other pirates clapped and whistled.

I was in complete pirate mode by this time as you know, and I really fancied boogieing with a pirate myself. Unfortunately Lola was almost falling asleep in her chair.

"Come on girlfriend," I sighed. "Time for some beauty sleep."

Brice had rented us two rooms for the night. My friend was so out of it that she let me support her as far as the door, then she shrugged me off.

The music had switched into something fiery and Spanish. I glanced back wistfully and saw Brice and

Mariah doing a lot of stamping and sexy peacock-type strutting. Two outlaws closing their deal in true outlaw style.

Who'd have imagined our maverick buddy would end up going into partnership with Cat Darcy's pirate granddaughter! In my wildest fantasies I couldn't come up with something like that.

I felt a flicker of excitement. Mel, this is WAY too karmic to be a coincidence, I told myself. OK, the Agency couldn't have known for sure, but they must have allowed for this mind-blowing possibility in their cosmic calculations.

And suddenly I was flooded with relief.

Omigosh, I thought, this was meant to happen! I'm NOT a failure! We were supposed to come to Port Royal and hook up with Mariah.

It totally didn't matter that I still hadn't managed to figure out a way to get my friends home. My friends weren't *supposed* to go home, because – omigosh, omigosh! – despite everything, we were still totally on track for Brice's HALO award!!!

I wanted to yodel like a sexy pirate girl. Instead I stood at the top of the stairs, fanning myself frantically, trying to absorb this amazingly good news.

Finally I'd calmed down enough to go into our room.

When I walked in, Lola muttered something I didn't catch and went on carefully pouring water into a cracked china bowl.

I have to say Diego's Whiskers wasn't exactly four-star accommodation. The bed curtains were visibly mouldy (euw!), and there were tiny lizards glued to the walls, looking like bizarre ornaments.

My friend leaned over the bowl to wash her face. Suddenly I saw something glint in the candlelight. My heart practically flew into my mouth. It was Lola's angel tags!

This was my chance.

Say something, Mel, I told myself. Say something NOW.

I cleared my throat. "Lola, this is going to sound like I'm making it up, but please hear me out, OK?"

I tried to explain what had happened in terms a seventeenth-century slave-girl could relate to, deliberately avoiding words like "Heaven" and "angel". If I hit her with the heavenly terminology right off, she'd think I was a nutter. So I just reminded my friend that the three of us came from a place where nobody went hungry and everything was free. In this wonderful country, slavery didn't exist.

"But something happened to you and Brice, erm Beau, on the way here," I explained. "Something that made you forget who you really are."

Lola yawned like a sleepy little cat. "Mi nah forget nuttin. You da one who confuse. You all di time talkin' wild-wild."

"I can prove it," I said eagerly. "When we leave our home to go travelling, we wear these." I showed Lola my tags. "See? They're exactly like yours."

She pulled a face. "Tcha! You can buy dem kinda ting in any slave market in Jamaica."

I was so disappointed. Whatever Lola was seeing, she wasn't seeing the same object. I could see she was completely exhausted so I let it go for the time being.

There was only one double bed in our room. Lola was all set to sleep on the floor, but I managed to persuade her we could share.

Before she went to sleep, my friend wrapped her sheet around her face and upper body. I guess she wanted to protect her face from prying eyes (mine) while she was sleeping. But it left her feet bare and vulnerable. I noticed a woven friendship bracelet around one ankle and felt my eyes fill with tears. I had made that bracelet for Lola one lazy afternoon in Heaven, a few weeks after we met.

I lay awake for a long time, listening to my soul-mate breathing softly inside her private cocoon. I could hear fiddle music and roars of laughter coming from downstairs. Plus some kind of drunken ruckus seemed to be going on in the alley outside.

After a few minutes I got up and wedged a chair under the door handle. Then I went back to bed and slept like a baby.

I must have gone back to Heaven in my dreams, because when I woke next morning, everything seemed clear. A little too clear, actually.

I had to giggle into my pillow so as not to wake my sleeping friend.

I couldn't believe I'd wanted to run off with the pirates! Some angel you are, Mel Beeby! I scolded myself.

After my sleep, I felt totally connected to the higher angelic realms. For once in my life, I knew exactly what I was going to do. I pictured myself walking down the corridor and knocking on

Brice's door. I pictured him appearing in the doorway with a wondering expression.

The true Brice was getting closer to the surface. I'd seen it in his eyes yesterday. If I went while I was zinging with angelic energy, I wouldn't have to worry about finding words. He'd look into my face and it would be like a light switching on. This bizarre illusion would vanish like a mirage and Brice would remember who and what he really was.

I knelt on our bed and peeped through the slatted window at the alley below. A drunken pirate sprawled face-down in the dirt. I couldn't see his face but I didn't think he was one of Mariah's. Chickens were carefully pecking around him. They probably saw this kind of thing all the time.

Do it Mel, I told myself.

I tiptoed out of our room in my petticoat and bare feet.

The door to Brice's room was wide open. A slave-girl was sweeping the floor, raising clouds of dust. Sunshine streamed through the window slats making the tiny dust specks dance in the light.

"Where's Mr Bexford?" I asked in dismay.

She shrugged. "Massa gone long time."

Brice had left while we were still sleeping.

He must have run off with Mariah Darcy to find Coyaba, City of the Gods.

# CHAPTER SEVEN

Lola sat on the edge of the bed clutching her raggedy bag full of smelly poisonous plants. She was shivering. She just went on sitting there shivering and staring emptily into space. After a while the bag slipped to the floor but she didn't seem to notice.

Two tiny lizards, no bigger than children's hairgrips, unglued themselves from the walls and skittered over to look at her in concern. They looked at me too, as if they were waiting for me to do something. But I just stood in the middle of the room, feeling useless.

What do you say to a runaway slave-girl when

the one white person she trusted abandons her without a word?

I was bitterly disappointed. I had put myself through the wringer to help Brice. Well, that jerk had just thrown away his last chance. And let's face it, he had had the MOST last chances.

No more sympathy for you, mister, I thought grimly. You have blown it, totally.

Being mad with Brice was quite therapeutic, but it didn't actually solve anything. In addition to her cosmic amnesia, my soul-mate was now utterly traumatised. To cap it all, we were stranded in Port Royal with absolutely no cash.

Mel Beeby, you are out of your depth with this one, I thought miserably. Michael offers to send in a SWAT team, but oh no. You have to know best.

The teeny lizards had skittered up one of the mildewed bed curtains. They clung there side by side, watching me and Lola with their beady bright eyes.

I was so upset, I went a bit mad. I started talking to the lizards in my head.

"Got any ideas?" I asked them miserably. "I'm not proud, you know. All suggestions gratefully received, believe me."

An ugly little bug flew past. Lizard Number One shot out its tongue and – bosh! – the bug was gone. Lizard Number Two went pattering down the curtain and across the floor. I thought it was hunting for an ugly bug of its own, but it kept pattering along until it reached my clothes. I'd dropped them in a heap the night before.

The lizard zoomed up the heap and froze dramatically at the top. You could almost hear it saying, "Ta-da!"

When I saw what it was standing *on*, I almost screamed. Can you believe I'd forgotten that purse?! A purse FULL of jewellery!

Omigosh, Melanie, I thought, everything's going to be OK!

Don't get me wrong. Jewels wouldn't mend Lola's broken heart. It wasn't the jewels that were making me so excited.

It was knowing I wasn't alone. I'd forgotten that really crucial heavenly messages always get through – via a lizard if necessary!

Of course, now that I'd remembered I was an angel, I was able to see my situation in a different way.

I felt a rush of shame as I realised I'd been doing exactly what angels are not supposed to do. I had judged our angel buddy without knowing the facts.

The fact is, Melanie, you DON'T know what happened last night, I reminded myself. OK, it looks like Brice has gone back to his bad old ways. It also looks like Lola and I aren't friends. And that's SO not true.

At that moment my friend looked up. "What mi do?" she asked in a trembling voice. "Mi cyan go back to Fruitful Vale. Mi cyan stay in dis wicked place. What mi do?"

I couldn't believe it. My friend was talking to me! She had actually asked for my help.

I didn't care that she didn't know who I was. I was much too grateful. Don't blow this Melanie, I told myself shakily.

This was the breakthrough I'd been waiting for.

I daringly sat down beside my traumatised friend. "It's going to be all right," I told her softly. "If your master went off without you, there's probably a good reason. Probably he thought it would be too dangerous."

Lola stared at me as if I'd started talking in Martian. "Too dangerous for me? Too dangerous for ME, a slave!" Then she completely exploded.

"Nuttin safe for slaves, NUTTIN!" Her face was quivering with rage and distress.

I was scared I was going to cry. Lola and I were only inches apart, yet there was this howling chasm between us. I wanted to make all her pain and suffering go away, but I didn't know how.

I groped blindly for words. "I know I don't understand what it's like to be a sl—"

Lola covered her face with her hands. I could hear gasping sounds.

The tiny soul-mate lizards were back on the wall, looking like they'd never moved. I got the feeling they were still watching. In a funny way those little lizards gave me courage.

I reached out to touch my friend, lost my nerve and pulled back. Tears spilled down my face.

"I'll never understand, will I?" I wept. "Oh, but Lola, I do *want* to."

My martial arts teacher says sometimes the hardest thing in the Universe is just to stay still. He says when we stop trying to fix everything and just stay still, we leave a space for miracles to happen.

Well that morning at Diego's, when Lola finally decided to trust me, I stayed still. Sometimes I wanted to run out of the room in pure horror at the things she was telling me. But I didn't. I didn't try to comfort her or make her feel better. I didn't try to make it into *my* story by nervously interrupting to explain that all white people weren't monsters. I just sat totally still and listened and it was truly the hardest thing I have ever done.

Lola wasn't really a slave, but I knew the things she was telling me were really true. And so I listened, not just with my ears, but with my whole hurting angel heart.

There was one time, though, when I wasn't able to keep quiet.

In a wistful voice, Lola was telling me how different Young Massa was to his uncle. Young Massa treated her with respect, not like pervy old Josiah, blatantly paying visits to the slave-women's huts at night.

"Ever see dem lickle yella-skin pickney runnin' round di plantation?" my friend asked abruptly. "Bright Eyes and dem?"

I figured "yella-skin pickney" meant "light-skinned children" and quickly nodded.

Lola gave me a meaningful look.

I was horrified. "You're not serious! Bright Eyes is old Master Bexford's little girl?"

"An' Jewel an' Precious." Lola gave a bleak little shrug. "Precious gone now. Ole Massa sell her las' month."

I had to wrap my arms around myself so as not to feel the ache inside. I thought of a slave mother choosing the most beautiful names she knew. I thought of her having to stand by helplessly as her master sold their little daughter like you'd sell a puppy. And I understood why Brice thought he had to buy the guns and ammunition.

When Lola finally stopped talking, it wasn't because she'd run out of stories, it was pure exhaustion.

I poured water into the bowl and washed my face. After checking carefully for lizards, I started struggling into my seventeenth-century clothes.

Lola looked stricken. "You go leave now, miss?"

I gave her a tired grin. "No babe, I'm taking you to breakfast."

It was more peaceful than you'd think in the courtyard at Diego's. The high walls kept out most of the street noise. Only sporadic gunshots in the distance reminded me we were in pirate territory. We were sitting in the shade of an old mango tree. Sunlight filtered through star-shaped leaves sending starry patterns flitting across our faces.

It was more like brunch than breakfast. It was past midday, but we seemed to be the only guests up and about. We didn't talk much. I think we both felt like limp rags. When we'd finished our roast breadfruit and ackee and saltfish, the girl came to see if we wanted anything else.

I had a sudden longing for something sweet. "I don't suppose you have hot chocolate?" I asked impulsively.

The hot chocolate at Diego's was so thick you practically had to eat it with a spoon. It smelled of nutmeg and cinnamon and something I couldn't place.

I kept catching Lola looking at me with a baffled expression. It was the same way she'd looked at me that day we first met in Heaven. Like she was thinking, who IS this girl?

I cleared my throat. "That place I told you about? We drink hot chocolate there all the time."

She gave me a wan smile. "Dey have streets pave wid gold in dat place too? Girl-chile, you always talkin' wild!"

"We're friends there," I insisted. "And no one thinks it's strange."

My friend sighed. "Dat place sound nice. Mi have a dream 'bout a place like dat."

I grabbed her hand. "Lola, I swear to you. It wasn't a dream!"

She shook her head vehemently. "Mi wake in dat stinking lickle hut, all bruise an' mash-up from Massa's beating. An' mi know dat other place not real."

I didn't ask Lola any more about her dream of Heaven. It was too painful for both of us.

And even if I could get a message back to the Agency, going back home was out of the question. We couldn't leave without Brice.

My friend and I sat at our table under the mango tree for a long time. Neither of us spoke, but it wasn't unfriendly.

And as we sat there, a daring plan formed in my mind.

I took a breath. "Last night, when they put the map on the table, I managed to get a look."

Lola sat up straight. "You know where dem go?"

"Not exactly. But that city isn't in the jungle, like people thought. It's in the middle of something called the Black Morass. No, sorry, the Black River Morass. Whatever a 'morass' is," I added sheepishly.

Lola shook her head. "Morass a bad ting. You get suck under di mud. Lungs jus' full up an'—" She made a graphic choking noise, rolling her eyes up into her head. "You dead."

"I thought it might mean that," I sighed. "Well, that's where the city is, so there you go."

Lola gasped. "Miss, bad duppy live in dat city!!"

"This entire island is full of bad duppy. Jamaica is practically built on dead people's bones! But we need to find Bri— erm, Beau Bexford, before something terrible happens."

My friend started to protest.

"Listen, babe," I said firmly, "as I see it, you've got three choices. Go back to Fruitful Vale and be beaten to death. Stay in Port Royal and wind up entertaining pervy pirates for a living. Euw!" I pulled a face at her. "Or, groovy Option Three, to join forces with the weird white girl, set off to find your boy Beau, and see what happens next."

After a while Lola looked up, her eyes dark with worry. "You tink Massa in danger?"

I pressed my hand to my chest. "I can feel it."

Lola nodded. "Mi feel it too." She leaned closer. "Las' night mi hear dat pirate girl tellin' Massa dey sail round di coast to a place where hill country start."

"Ooh, Lola!" I teased her. "I thought you were asleep!"

She gave a sly giggle. "Hear more tings dat way."

"Can you remember what the place was called?"

Lola shook her head ruefully. "It drop outa mi head."

I had a flash of inspiration. Angels have brilliant photographic memories, plus Mr Allbright makes us play angelic observation games all the time. I'd never had to do this exercise under pressure, but if I could remember the name of this place, we'd have a landmark for the starting point of our journey.

I shut my eyes, trying to recreate the blood-stained map fragments in my mind's eye. It worked. I could see the coastline with total clarity. Unfortunately I had no idea which landmark was the crucial one. I was on the verge of panicking when, for absolutely no reason, song lyrics floated up from the bottom of my mind. A song Lola put on tape for me, for when I needed a boost: *Sisters are Doing it for Themselves.* I mentally scanned along the Jamaican coastline, and there it was!

"Three Sisters," I said abruptly. "Three Sisters Cave."

Lola clapped. "Dat di one!"

Lola and I went back to our room. We couldn't exactly tell anyone the real reason we needed to go to Three Sisters Cave, so we cooked up a story about how my childhood sweetheart was waiting for me somewhere on the beach nearby. I know it sounds a bit dodgy, but people married really young in those days.

It took ages to make the wording of my tale of True Love seem convincingly natural, but finally we were ready to check out.

Before we went back out into the real world, I wanted to make something totally clear.

"Everyone out there will assume you're my slave," I said.

Lola quickly lowered her eyes. "Yes, miss."

"Stuff 'yes miss'!" I said fiercely. "'Yes miss', is

banned for ever. My point is, you and I know different. From now on we're partners."

Lola opened her mouth.

"Partners," I repeated firmly. I gave one last glance around our room. "Don't you want your herbs?" I said in surprise.

Lola had left her withered collection of poisonous plants on the bed.

She just shook her head.

I gave a nervous laugh. "Does that mean you've stopped wanting to poison me?"

My friend shook her head again. "Mi nah poison you, girl-chile."

I was genuinely touched. "Really?"

Lola's eyes glinted. "Where we goin', dey got alligators!"

We went down to the docks and asked around for a boat to take us to Three Sisters Cave. Every person we spoke to looked blank and passed us on to someone else. Off we'd trudge to another sleazy waterfront location and I'd tell our story again.

It got really boring hearing myself repeat the same thing over and over. After a while, Lola and I started adding colourful touches.

My sweetheart and I were to be married as soon as he got his inheritance. Meanwhile my evil uncle was in hot pursuit. My wicked uncle had wanted to marry me off to his pervy best friend, but I was determined to marry my true love.

At last someone directed us to a boat called the *Susannah*. When we got there the *Susannah* turned out to be a full-sized sailing ship. Dirty and dilapidated, but way too grand for what we had in mind.

I was going to say we'd try somewhere else, when a sharp-eyed deckhand came dashing down the gangplank. "You the young mistress wants to hire a boat?"

Wow, news travels fast in Port Royal, I thought. The deckhand had actually been told to look out for us! A minute later we were on board, talking to the captain!

I have to say Captain Plum didn't exactly fit my picture of a sea captain. He was quite old and his clothes were greasy and grimy. There were icky bits of food in his beard and his eyes were red-rimmed from drinking too much rum. But as I told my story he made sympathetic noises in all the right places. When I'd finished, he shook his head as if he couldn't believe what this world was coming to.

"I can pay," I said quickly. "My uncle didn't take all my jewellery."

The captain looked thoughtful. "We're bound for Hispaniola on the next tide. We shall be sailing past the very landmark where your young man is waiting."

I felt a prickle of excitement. "That's fantastic! Does that mean you'll take us!"

Captain Plum put his head on one side like a wise old bird. "Did I hear you say you had a little jewellery, young mistress? I'd gladly take you for free, but I'm not getting any younger and times are hard."

I kept back a sweet little bracelet for emergencies, and poured the rest into the captain's hands. This was such a cool way of doing business! Way more romantic than cash or credit cards.

It seemed like we'd only just found the *Susannah* in time. Just minutes later, her rusty old anchor was hauled up dripping on to the deck. Her sails filled with a rush of wind and, with mighty creaks and groans, the battered old sailing vessel eased away from the waterfront.

As we sailed away from Port Royal, I couldn't stop smiling.

You're finally losing it, babe, I told myself. There is absolutely nothing to smile about. May I just remind you that we don't actually have a map!

Could two angels find their way through the Black River Morass without a map? I had no idea. Could we track Brice down before he helped to plunder a sacred city and blew his final last chance of having a career as an angel? I didn't know that either. All I knew was that my friend and I were a team again. We had made a plan and we had followed it through. Now we were on a seventeenth-century sailing ship watching pelicans fly home to their nests, or wherever pelicans sleep at nights.

I was SO happy I started humming our *Sisters* theme tune. This is what Mariah means about being free, I thought. Life is so-o much more fun if you just go for it!

Lola and I watched the whole sunset from beginning to end, until the sun vanished into the sea in a final fabulous blaze of colour.

The ship sailed on through a deep blue dusk. I could see glittery trails of phosphorescence on the water. I became vaguely aware that the sweet greenhousey smells of Jamaica were fading. There were just smells of rope and tar and sea salt. Instead of hugging the Jamaican coastline, the *Susannah* was heading out to sea.

Lola looked bewildered. "What happen?"

"It's fine," I told her cheerfully. "The sailors are just trying to avoid rocks or something. They'll correct their course in a few minutes."

I heard stealthy creaking sounds. A man with a knife between his teeth swung himself up on deck, landing as softly as a cat.

Before we could raise the alarm, a dozen or so hard-faced men came swarming over the side. At the same moment, a galleon flying a sinister black flag loomed out of the dusk.

The *Susannah* been captured by pirates!

# CHAPTER EIGHT

The *Susannah*'s crew stood by sullenly as the pirates swept through the ship, tearing open hatches, taking trunks, crates and boxes.

They jemmied open one of the boxes and I was astonished to see precious metals glittering inside. Apparently Captain Plum was some kind of smuggler. But when they found the guns and barrels of gunpowder, I was genuinely shocked. Was there *anyone* who wasn't a pirate in Jamaica?

A young black buccaneer was supervising the pillaging, setting up a chain gang to pass the loot up from below, making sure his men didn't miss anything crucial. He had his hair tightly braided into hundreds of gleaming plaits and he wore a rich crimson waistcoat over a baggy white shirt. The sleeves glimmered in the Caribbean dusk. I have to say he was really good-looking; well, if you go for gangster types.

I heard him talking angrily to Captain Plum at one point, but I was too confused and scared to take it in. The *Susannah*'s captain wasn't exactly the friendly character I'd thought.

All the pirates carried knives or evil-looking cutlasses, except the pirate chief – he had a sword with a jewel-encrusted hilt. For backup, he had two pairs of pistols hanging at the end of a silk sling over his shoulders.

He only spoke when necessary and I never saw him actually hurt anyone. Yet each time he came close, I instinctively backed away. He gave off this totally electric vibe. The vibe of someone with absolutely nothing to lose.

The pirates brought their ship, the *Santa Rosa* alongside the *Susannah* and two of her crew wedged a plank between the decks.

Lola and I watched in amazement as the pirates performed a reckless trapeze act, ferrying huge trunks and crates across this madly wobbling bridge as if they were just popping next door.

When the last boxes had been taken on to his ship, the pirate chief gestured to me and Lola. "Now make haste, pretty ladies."

I looked helplessly at Captain Plum. Surely he wouldn't allow us to be abducted by dangerous buccaneers?

To my dismay he just exploded. "Do what he says, wench! And take the slave-girl with you!"

Seconds later I was inching across the plank, trying not to look down. I could hear Lola's scared breathing behind me and the swoosh of waves far below. I told myself it was a good thing it was dark. I'd never know if those were actual sharks circling below or purely imaginary ones.

The minute we tottered on to the deck, the *Santa Rosa*'s pirates surrounded us like hungry hyenas.

Of all the times for Mr Allbright's words to come back to me. *Pirates were not sweet, Melanie... They were calculating, cold-blooded murderers...*

I felt as if the whole world had turned upside down. I couldn't imagine why they'd kidnapped us. Did we look like people who have gold and jewels stashed away? A deeply unpleasant thought crept into my mind. I hope it's not because we're girls, I thought nervously, and they want to—

Suddenly I was gabbling at top speed. "I think there's been a mistake. We aren't rich. All I've got left is—"

I groped wildly for my purse. There was just a severed cord hanging from my waist. A tousle-haired pirate cabin boy waved my purse cheekily from a nearby ladder. He pulled out the bracelet and bit it to test the gold.

"We are not common thieves!" The pirate captain yanked the boy off the ladder, cuffed him round the ear and returned my bracelet with a bow.

"Leo hasn't been with us long. He gets carried away," he explained apologetically. "Allow me to introduce myself. I am Rufus Valentine, captain of the *Santa Rosa*." He chuckled. "At least I am now!"

I looked at the rough-looking men in earrings and bandannas, and at the stacked boxes and barrels they'd taken from the *Susannah*. Then I stared up at the ominous black flag flapping in the evening breeze. Even the ship had been stolen by all accounts.

"I'm sorry," I said, "but you look like thieves to me."

Captain Valentine gave another low chuckle. "We're thieves, little mistress! Just not *common* thieves."

"Oh, right, my favourite kind," I said angrily. "I suppose you steal from the rich and give to the poor?"

His smile faded. "I am not so noble as your Robin of the Woods. But villains who prey on helpless females deserve to be taught a lesson."

I felt like I was missing something. "I'm sorry?"

"I am afraid you were too open about your personal affairs. Every water rat in Port Royal has heard that your fiancé is to come into a large inheritance. The captain of the *Susannah* was going to keep you hostage and demand a ransom for your return."

I stared at him. "You're telling me you *rescued* us?"

He gave another deep bow. "I was honoured to be of service."

I don't think I have ever felt so stupid. Our story had rebounded in the worst way.

"But in the future it would be wise to be a little more discreet," Captain Valentine suggested.

I could feel my face burning but I knew I'd better come clean. "Erm, actually, there is no inheritance. We made that up. There is no fiancé either."

The pirate raised an eyebrow. "Then why did you charter the *Susannah*?"

Great, he doesn't believe me, I thought.

"It's kind of personal," I told him.

"It must be something important," the pirate said softly, "for you to put yourself and your slave in such danger."

"It is important," I said. "And Lola's not my slave. Look, everything isn't always about money, OK? There is NO fiancé. And there is NO inheritance. If you rescued us to do Captain Plum out of the ransom, you're out of luck. That bracelet your little sonny boy pinched just now, is all we have left in the world."

The pirate looked astonished. "Mistress, did you think—"

"You know what," I interrupted angrily, "Columbus should have stayed at home to raise pigs and done everyone a favour!"

"Pigs?" he echoed in a bewildered voice.

"Everything's been galloping downhill since he came to the Caribbean. Everyone wants a piece of whatever is going and no one cares who they hurt to get it. Well I've HAD it with the New World. I've had it up to here!"

A stunned silence descended. The pirate ship was so hushed I could literally hear Lola's teeth chattering. She probably thought we were going to be fed to the sharks. All the pirates were totally riveted. I think they were dying to know what would happen next.

Nothing did for several nerve-wracking moments. I'd just decided to beam some uplifting vibes quick-smart, when Captain Valentine did something I totally didn't expect.

He took off his beautiful waistcoat and draped it respectfully around my shivering friend's shoulders. "The night air is cool, little sister," he told her, "and your dress is thin. I suggest we go below."

He gave me a cool smile. "I do not want your ransom, mistress. You and your friend are my guests. My crew and I are humbly at your service."

I followed the captain in a daze. A pirate who rescued females in distress? Was Captain Valentine for real?

But when I saw the captain's private quarters, my jaw absolutely dropped. It was gorgeous! Everywhere you looked there was something beautiful, an exotic rug, a silk hanging, a painting. Shelves were crammed with leather-bound books, several written in foreign languages. They weren't just for show. He had what looked like a poetry book lying open on his desk.

"Please," he said. "Make yourselves comfortable."

Lola and I seated ourselves self-consciously on a wooden settle.

"You are now under my protection," he said gravely.

"OK," I squeaked.

"I give you my word you will come to no harm," he went on. "I would very much like to help you."

Some people would say a pirate's word wasn't worth much. Obviously I didn't trust Captain Valentine an inch. Though he was incredibly charming. Lots of people are charming, Mel, I reminded myself. Especially if it gets them what they want.

On the other hand, did I have a choice? I asked myself.

I took a major risk. I told Rufus Valentine everything that had happened, carefully leaving out references to angels or amnesia. I'm afraid I totally got on my soapbox when I described the treatment of the slaves on my uncle's plantation. And after that Lola started shyly chipping in. She'd obviously decided to trust the pirate chief too, and this Lola was not the trusting type, as you know. It started feeling just like old times with both of us talking at once and setting each other straight. I could see this really amused him.

We told Captain Valentine about hot-headed Beau Bexford and his outrageous scheme to set the Fruitful Vale slaves free. And we described how Bermuda Jack had sold my cousin part of a map showing the whereabouts of an ancient Taino city. "It's SO bizarre," I said. "Beau is incredibly respectful of Taino culture, yet he seems to think it's cool to rip off their gold just so long as it's in a good cause." I gave Lola a stern look. "And before you say anything, babe, I KNOW it's dead people's gold, OK? But it just doesn't seem right."

We told the captain how the three of us left Fruitful Vale at dead of night and rode off to Port

Royal to find the mysterious owner of the map's other half.

The captain shook his head at me. "You clearly have a relish for danger, little mistress," he said, with a straight face. "I had no idea I was rescuing an adventuress."

"The most dangerous thing on the journey was Lola," I giggled. "She wanted to poison me."

Lola made her eyes wide and innocent. "Mi never poison you. Mi jus' pick mi lickle herbs dem, and look at you, like dis!" She shot me an evil look under her brows, then creased up laughing.

The pirate looked uneasy when I mentioned Mariah Darcy, but he listened attentively until I had finished. Then he got up to pace.

"So Mistress Mariah is mixed up in this," he said.

"You know her!" I was suddenly intrigued.

"I knew her at one time," he said rather grimly. "But I did not like the company she keeps." He sighed. "I am afraid your cousin will not find his gold. This worries me. I have heard of this city and it is precious, but for reasons Mistress Darcy and her kind will never understand."

"Oh she isn't interested in the gold!" I said eagerly. "Mariah said if they found gold, he could keep it to save the..."

The captain and Lola were staring at me as if I was bonkers.

"She was lying, wasn't she?" I said in a small voice.

"When Mariah wants something badly, she can make you believe ashes are stardust." He twiddled one of his braids thoughtfully. "I suppose you didn't get a look at that map?"

"We think the city is hidden in something called the Black River Morass," I said. "And we're fairly sure Mariah was heading for a landing place near Three Sisters Cave."

"I know it. I'll take you there at first light. It will take at least two days to reach the Morass, going through Cockpit Country."

"Isn't that where rebel slaves hide out?" I asked.

Captain Valentine looked evasive. "So they say. But I have heard many strange stories about those hills. People say that when the soldiers come with muskets and hunting dogs, things happen which cannot be explained. Out of nowhere, the mist comes down and the men find themselves walking in circles. They stumble into bogs or fall into ravines. Their dogs mysteriously go missing. Yet a slave can hide in those hills for weeks and months and never be found. So I have heard."

My arms had come out in goosebumps. "You make it sound like the country is alive," I told him. "Like it's deliberately taking the slaves under its protection."

"It feels like that sometimes." The pirate's voice sounded dreamy and far away. Then his mood changed abruptly. "But you young ladies are under *my* protection. Tonight *I* shall draw you a map of the quickest and safest route through the hills."

I suddenly understood something about Captain Valentine, and I was shocked to the core.

"You were there!" I said. "You were hiding, while the soldiers blundered around in the mist. You were a runaway slave."

Lola gave me a look and I saw that she had known all along. I had done that ugly European thing again, talking about things I couldn't begin to understand.

I started to apologise, but the pirate was already speaking.

"Yes," he said quietly. "I was a slave. I belonged to a white man by the name of George Wainwright Valentine. When I was six years old I saw George Valentine beat a young man to death for daring to look him in the eyes. I vowed then that I would run away as soon as I was grown."

"Omigosh, how can you bear to use that man's name?" I said in horror. "You aren't a slave any more. Why ever don't you choose a new name?"

To my amazement he smiled. "I have earned 'Valentine'. I have worn it like a second-hand boot. I have stretched and worked at it over the years, until it stopped pinching and became mine. I never knew my true name or my true parents. I don't even know what language they spoke. The very words I use, I borrow from books written by white men."

When I first saw Rufus Valentine I felt scared of him because I guessed he was a man with nothing to lose. I hadn't realised he'd lost everything before he was even born.

He seemed to know what I was thinking.

"Yes, little mistress," he said softly. "The world can be harsh. Yet still, it is good to be alive!"

We slept in a spare cabin on silk sheets which Captain Valentine insisted had belonged to a Spanish Infanta.

The tousle-haired cabin boy woke us at sunrise. "The captain says to bring you these," he grinned.

He had brought us a bundle of old but perfectly clean clothes. Stripy cotton tops, pirate bandannas to protect our heads from the sun, and breeches drastically faded by salt and sun.

Yay! I can finally ditch that corset, I thought gratefully.

To my surprise, Lola chose the blue top and bandanna, so obviously I took the red. I didn't say anything but I couldn't help being puzzled. Lola's slave clothes were blue. You'd think she'd be desparate for a change. But it was like she felt safer sticking to something she knew.

We creased up laughing when we saw each other in our pirate gear.

But I felt a happy little buzz. In our matching clothes, we finally looked like equals. We looked as if we could actually be friends.

We went to say our goodbyes to Captain Valentine.

He seemed genuinely sorry to see us go. "I advise you to get out of sight as soon as you reach dry land. The militia watch this part of the coast like hawks, and the *Santa Rosa* is a Spanish vessel. If they see you in those clothes they will shoot first and ask questions afterwards."

He raised my fingers to his lips. "Farewell, little mistress."

OK, so it was just a charming gesture, plus he kissed Lola's hand immediately afterwards, but ooh la la! Say what you like about this mission, I thought, but we are certainly seeing life!

We clambered down a rope ladder to a waiting dinghy. As we pulled away from the *Santa Rosa*, I waved shyly to Captain Valentine.

Our pirate boatman spoke practically no English. He rowed us as close as he could get without running aground, then solemnly handed us two small bundles that obviously contained food.

I wondered what Mr Allbright would think if he knew we had met yet another pirate with a heart. Handsome Captain Valentine had been for real after all. He had even drawn us a map to help us reach the Black River Morass.

We splashed ashore and scrambled quickly up the rocks and out of sight, in case the English militia were watching from some secret outpost.

The first part of our journey took us through rocky hills where nothing grew but scrub and cactus. The barren landscape gradually gave way to coconut palms and rippling fields of sugar cane.

At midday we stopped to rest in the shade of a palm tree, and ate some of our pirate provisions. The ship's cook had packed tiny hard-boiled eggs and strips of dried meat and a type of flat bread which Lola said was made from cassava root.

When we'd finished lunch, we wandered around for a while like happy little kids, picking tropical fruit and berries. Lola picked a fruit she called "sweet sop". It didn't look that special but it was gorgeous. You broke open the shell and there was this delicious natural custard inside. I caught Lola watching me as I slurped at this unexpected treat.

"What?" I said.

My friend's eyes were dreamy and unfocused, almost as if she was seeing *through* me to someone or somewhere else.

"Nuttin," she said softly. "Just tinkin' 'bout dat dream city you talk 'bout."

I got a tingly feeling inside. Lola's memory was coming back, I was sure of it. But I didn't want to push her before she was ready, so I just said, "Oh that's all right. I thought maybe I was dribbling down my chin."

That afternoon we kept up a cracking pace, despite the intense heat. By sunset we had reached the foot of some really peculiar hills. They looked like upside-down puddings with hollowed-out depressions in between.

I saw Lola's face light up. "See dem lickle valleys. Dey look jus' like cockfightin' pits! Mus' be why dey call dis Cockpit Country, eh?"

I'd never seen cocks fighting, but it had to be gruesome. I suppressed a shiver. "You could be right."

"Ole Massa Bexford jus' love cockfightin'," Lola remembered. "A whole heap a dem white massas come over and dey make di poor birds fight-fight till one dead. Mi watch one time, but it make mi spit up everyting in mi belly."

But as we stood there, mopping sweat from our faces and gazing at the amazing view, all the cruel goings-on at Fruitful Vale seemed like a bad dream.

"Slaves call dis place nutha name some time," my friend said, almost whispering the words. "Dem call it di Land of Look Behind."

"The Land of Look Behind," I repeated. It sounded like a place in a story.

I felt so proud of us I can't tell you. Lola and I had been abandoned in a violent city without any money, without even a map. We'd been tricked by pirates and captured by a totally different set of pirates. Yet here we were in the foothills of the Land of Look Behind, in hot pursuit of our angel buddy.

It was going to be dark, so we found a guango tree with spreading umbrella-type branches, and made a rough kind of camp. We piled up dry leaves for a mattress (first checking for snakes!). Lola lit a fire and we shared our pirate rations.

In a movie, this would be the scene where the two angel girls end up having a meaningful talk in the firelight, shed some tears and finally iron out their misunderstandings.

In a movie, though, they'd leave out the mosquitoes. I doubt even Albert Einstein could have had a meaningful conversation with vicious bloodsucking insects attacking exposed bits of his anatomy. Actually, I have this theory. I think mosquitoes adore angels! I think we're like this amazing cosmic delicacy, that they totally can't have too much of. Lola and I did *try* to talk, but we had to keep interrupting each other with frantic slapping sounds.

I started to think we'd be swatting mozzies until daybreak. But when you've been walking in the open air from dawn till dusk, pure exhaustion takes over.

Lola and I gradually slid down until we were lying under our guango-tree umbrella. The whine of mosquitoes began to mix itself into an atmospheric soundtrack, along with chirping crickets, tree frogs and soothing rippling sounds from a nearby stream. I could see showers of tiny stars dancing in the dark. Melanie this is so cool, you're finally seeing fireflies, I thought drowsily. I wanted to stay awake watching the tiny magic dancing lights, but my eyes kept closing.

I wondered where Brice was and if he was watching fireflies with Mariah Darcy. It was so weird the way he'd left us in Port Royal like that. Weird and deeply worrying. I truly tried not to think the worst, but I had this horrible suspicion that our night with the pirates had brought out our buddy's dark side.

Look at the effect they had on you, Melanie, I told myself. And you're a complete wuss.

In the movie of our lives, I would have fallen fast asleep at this point and had a dream that told me exactly what was going on for Brice.

But my dreams seemed every bit as confused as waking life. Brice was standing on some crumbling stone steps in the moonlight, watching Mariah's pirates loading fabulous Taino treasures into canoes.

In my dreams he wore normal clothes and looked just like he did in real life, hands in pockets, collar up round his ears. Same lonely, complicated Brice.

"You should be happy, angel boy," I told him. "You found the city."

Brice looked sick with fear. "There's been a mistake," he told me. He pointed to a huge carving of a Taino god that was towering over us like some ancient tree. The god's carved face wore an expression of deep suffering.

"Omigosh, it's got tears," I said in surprise.

At that moment the carved tears became real. They streamed down the wooden face of the god. By the time they reached the ground they'd become a torrent, thundering through the city, sweeping away temples, pirates, canoes and treasures.

I woke screaming, "I'm sorry! I didn't mean to!"

Lola was staring down at me in concern. "What happen?"

"I just had a bad dream. I'm OK honestly."

Lola lay down again.

After a while I felt her hand grope for mine.

We slept like that, hand in hand, until morning.

Some dreams hover over you all the next day like the wings of a sinister bird. You can still see sunlight and blue sky. You go about your business as normal, yet your dream casts a shadow you totally can't ignore.

I loved Cockpit Country. I absolutely loved the round pudding-shaped hills. I loved how green everything was. The sheer variety of trees and flowers blew me away. Palm trees with silver leaves. Vivid blue morning glories and golden black-eyed susans.

One time, Lola silently pointed out a plantation of yams obviously being cultivated in one of the fertile "cockpits" between the hills. A shiver of happiness went through me to think I'd seen a secret garden tended by runaway slaves.

I especially loved the yams. They looked oddly alive. It was almost spooky. Like green giants that might uproot themselves any minute and go galumphing over the hills.

But most of all I loved that Lola and I were getting reacquainted.

She still wasn't totally my Lola, but she was excellent company all the same. She took everything in her stride. Nothing fazed her, not even when I got confused by Captain Valentine's map. We must have wasted a good hour before we got back on track, but Lola said philosophically, "So it go!"

One time I fell in the stream and soaked myself to the skin. Lola laughed so much she almost fell in herself.

But lurking under these happy moments, like disturbing music in a film, were the dark vibes from my dream. They made things feel not quite real:

like this was just a holiday from the horrors of real life.

And as you know, holidays can't last.

Towards the end of the afternoon, we were making our way through a deep valley, knee-deep in lush green ferns and wild flowers. There was dense thicket on either side. Somewhere a bird was singing for pure joy.

I'm not sure that is a bird actually, I thought.

At the same moment I heard the tiniest twig-crack. Lola froze. By then it was too late.

We were surrounded by half-naked humans brandishing spears.

Lola and I were too shocked to move. Who were these flat-faced dark-skinned people? They weren't slaves. They weren't like any people I'd seen in Jamaica. Yet I felt I had seen them before.

When you're scared, random things jump out at you. I found myself focusing for no reason on their headdresses and jewellery. The elaborate collars and amulets were made from shimmery seashells, cut so cleverly they could have been precious gems. The exotic feathers braided in their hair made them seem magical, almost childlike; the kind of people who might have existed when the world was new and simple.

I hadn't seen these people because they were practically extinct. I was looking at the last survivors of the Taino.

# CHAPTER NINE

There were seven canoes altogether, gliding through the water as silently as shadows. We shared a canoe with the chief's grandson, a boy called Marohu, and a wiry little dog with alert pointy ears.

We were going to Coyaba, the City of the Gods, and something huge was going to happen there.

I had asked the chief if it was a good something, or something bad, but he had just shaken his head. "Something hard," he said quietly.

We paddled down silent backwaters, between steep banks lush with ferns and orangey-gold black-eyed susans. After an hour we reached a place where three rivers met and went speeding out into wide open water. I could hear tropical birds calling to each other high in the trees.

Marohu looked rigid with nerves. I couldn't blame him. Who'd want to be in a canoe with the Angel of Death?

That was me, in case you're wondering. The Taino chief had been expecting me. He wasn't called a "chief" by the way. Strictly speaking he was a *cacique*, (it actually sounded like *kaseek)*. That meant he was like the leader of the tribe and a holy man all rolled into one. He hadn't been expecting *me* in person. He wasn't looking out specifically for an angel-girl called Mel Beeby. I was more like a sign: *She who Flew on the Wings of the Storm*. The final sign their world was ending.

You know how it is, you're trying to lighten the atmosphere, so you chat madly about anything that comes into your head. I focused on the dog, the way you do. How sweet it was, how well-behaved, its perky little ears.

Ma:ohu gradually relaxed. He told me his dog was called Beetle. Like all Taino dogs, Beetle was barkless. "Better for hunting," he explained shyly. "Barking dogs scare the animals."

Lola looked baffled when I translated this conversation.

"How you can speak to dese people?" she hissed. "How dey know you?"

"I have no idea, babe," I said truthfully. "But where we come from, we understand all the human languages."

It probably seems like I was taking this really calmly?

I didn't have a choice. To the Taino, I was a messenger from their gods. This wasn't a part I'd have chosen, obviously. That wasn't the point. Mysterious cosmic forces were clearly at work and I felt I had to go with the flow.

Luckily it's hard to take yourself too seriously when your face is being licked by a rapturous Taino hunting dog.

Marohu was mortified. He kept saying he didn't know what had got into her. Normally Beetle was as good as gold. But I knew she couldn't help it. The poor little thing was just overexcited by our angelic vibes.

"Is a dream, dis," Lola murmured to herself. "Soon mi wake. Mi wake an' hear Quashiba singin' in she hut."

It seemed like a dream to me too; travelling in a canoe with a boy from a tribe that was about to vanish for ever.

We sped down the wide river under a green canopy of leaves, until the sun sank low in the sky. At a sign from the old cacique, the Taino lifted their canoes out of the water. The men slung hammocks between palm trees and lit a fire. One of the Taino had been catching fresh-water fish. The men gutted the fish, wrapped them in some kind of aromatic leaves, impaled them on sharp wooden skewers and baked them over the fire. Tricky to eat with fingers, and just a teensy bit too hot, but ooh, so dee-licious! There was cassava cake to fill any empty spaces and coconut water to wash it down.

Afterwards the cacique asked to speak with me. He was really old; in his eighties, maybe even his nineties. His eyesight was bad, and he must have been stiff and tired after hours in a canoe, yet I could feel this amazing vibe coming from him. I got the strangest feeling that he knew who I was. I mean *really* knew. In fact, I started wondering if this wise old man might be some kind of earth angel.

He started by telling me about Coyaba, the City of the Gods. For thousands of years, he said, native people travelled there in canoes from all over the Caribbean to honour their gods.

After Columbus discovered the Caribbean, this all changed. His people were initially willing to live with white people in peace, but there were so many of them; they came like hordes of locusts, and they seemed to want to own Xaymaca in a way the Taino totally didn't understand. How could you own trees or birdsong?

The Europeans forced the Taino to work in their fields. Some actually hunted the tribespeople for sport. Many died of the white man's diseases. Others killed themselves in despair. Soon only a few were left, hiding out in the hills.

"Yet still the location of the sacred city was fiercely protected," the cacique told me. "Each generation of Taino memorised the secret route, passing it down from generation to generation."

I was feeling increasingly uncomfortable.

"It isn't really made of gold, though, is it?"

For the first time the old man seemed irritated, as if I was missing the point. "Ah those mysterious golden cities," he sighed. "Soon my people will vanish like a bird trail in the sky, and all the gold in creation will not bring us back."

"I – I hate to tell you this, but I think someone's betrayed you," I said miserably. "Someone drew a map of the route. I saw it in Port Royal. A friend of mine got hold of one half. Someone called Mariah Darcy has the other."

The cacique sighed. "I have heard of this young woman. And what I hear worries me greatly. So much intelligence and beauty, yet inside she feels empty. Always hungering for something she can't have."

"That's too harsh," I objected. "Mariah is—"

"Your friend on the other hand," the old man continued firmly, "is descended from a long line of rats' arses."

(Sorry, he might not have said "rats' arses" exactly, but it's the closest word I can get to the Taino.)

I stared at him, open-mouthed. "You *know* about Brice?"

"Rats' *arses*," he repeated in a louder voice. "Yet his soul shines like moonbeams on water."

My heart was thumping. "You think Brice is in danger, don't you!"

The cacique's eyes were troubled. "Evil hovers over this boy like the wings of a vulture. I ask myself, 'Why are these dark beings going to so much trouble to destroy him? He must have made them very angry.'"

It was a warm night, but I could feel chills going up and down my back.

"Your friend lived in utter darkness. Yet he found the strength to leave. Such souls have a rare power. They are not afraid of the world's dark places. They shine light on them."

I didn't quite buy the cacique's version of an angel loner who sat around listening to Astral Garbage CDs. I opened my mouth to tell him that at this moment his precious shining light was looting his sacred city to buy guns.

But the old man's next words sent a jolt of fear into my heart.

"That is why the Dark Forces are trying to destroy him. They are playing with him. They have been playing with you all."

When I went back, Lola was fast asleep.

As I lay rigid in my hammock, totally traumatised by what I'd heard, Lola spoke to me. "I wish I could see this place," she whispered. "I should love to speak all the languages like you."

My skin prickled with angel electricity.

Lola had spoken in her normal voice.

We were on our way well before it was light.

We had breakfast on the move, nibbling at flat cassava bread as we went along. I gave most of mine to Beetle. I was too edgy to eat.

I wanted to ask Lola if she remembered talking to me in her sleep, but Marohu was there, plus my friend seemed tired and preoccupied.

For the first two hours the river was fast and deep-flowing. Then it divided off into an absolute maze of channels that wandered off, looping and crisscrossing the boggy flood plains, looking like some nightmarish brainteaser: *Find Your Way to the Sacred City*. Tortured-looking mangrove trees reared up out of the water forcing Marohu to paddle around them. We had now entered the Morass itself. When I saw how skilfully the Taino guided their canoes along the secret waterways, I realised I'd been insane to think we could find Coyaba on our own.

The Morass wasn't black, it was slimy green and

brown. After just an hour in this place, I started to feel like these were the only colours left in the world. Sludgy brown water, greenish-brown reeds, slimy sinister trees.

Since my scary talk with the cacique, I'd had the sense of being watched by something evil. Here, in this unbelievably creepy place, I felt the Dark Powers coming closer.

Everything about the Morass was sinister: the steamy suffocating air, the sinister screechy birds that we never actually saw, but sounded huge. Ominous bubbling, sucking sounds were literally coming from inside the swamp. Worst of all were the writhing mangrove roots that looked like agonised body parts of people who had been buried alive, and who died struggling to get free. And over it was this all-pervading stink of rotting vegetation and marsh gas.

Suddenly there was an explosion of sound. An alligator shot out of the reeds and came speeding towards us like a torpedo. Marohu paddled us frantically out of reach.

After my heartbeat returned to normal, I still found myself seeing those cold yellow eyes. Had it truly been an alligator? Or something worse?

And then, without warning, it was over. Marohu just stopped paddling and our canoe glided silently into a lake.

It was like going from darkness into light. Birds sang. A soft breeze trembled through the fronds of palm trees. And tiny white clouds reflected back in the clear, still waters of the lake.

Marohu paddled the canoe towards a towering cliff where a ledge of rock made a natural landing stage. From here you could see a flight of steps in the rock face. We helped Marohu drag the canoe out of the water, then followed the Taino up the steps.

At the top was the entrance to what looked like a large cave, but was actually the entrance to a tunnel. On either side of the entrance were enormous wooden pillars carved with images of the Taino gods.

A shiver went through me as I recognised the weeping god I had seen in my dream. I wanted to run, but I couldn't. This wasn't about me. I wasn't an individual to the Taino. I was the angel of their Last Days. I was *She who Flew on the Wings of the Storm*. I took a deep breath and followed the others into the tunnel.

The cacique walked ahead of us holding up a burning torch. I saw dim, ancient paintings flickering on the smooth rock face. They looked like birds and animals. But I think they were also gods. There were more steps at the end of this tunnel. We climbed and climbed in the flickering gloom until my legs were on the verge of giving out. Then we emerged in the sunlight and there were no words.

I saw my own wonder and astonishment reflected in Lola's face.

She had seemed in a kind of trance since we'd joined forces with the Taino. But as we finally stood inside the City of the Gods, I felt something change. I felt her start to wake up.

Listen, I can tell you what we saw. I can tell you about the actual physical stuff we saw in the City of the Gods. I could list Taino houses, gardens and fountains. I could describe the huge open space with benches, where the Taino used to play an incomprehensible sacred game that makes absolutely no sense if you're not Taino. I could get all lyrical about the carvings encrusted with shimmering seashells and all that jazz.

That would be missing the point. This stuff – the playing field, the quaint Taino objects, their fabulous flair for working with shells – was not what made the city so magical. You couldn't just carry off their *stuff* and knock up a sacred city of your own.

Can you imagine somewhere, *anywhere*, on Planet Earth where you can just breathe in pure peace? Where you can just, like, mingle with invisible gods? The awesome power of this place made me tingle all over.

We were walking slowly towards a small shimmering Taino temple. It seemed to be constructed entirely out of mother-of-pearl seashells.

I thought of how the first white men who came to Jamaica used to hunt the Taino for sport, as if they were animals!

We've got to save this place, I thought suddenly. People have to see this. They have to know how incredibly wise the Taino really are.

I was going to say something, but one of the Taino gestured fiercely for everyone to stay quiet.

When I saw what was happening inside that beautiful little temple, I had to bite my lip to stop myself crying out.

One of Mariah's men was kicking angrily at the base of a shrine, scattering shimmery shell fragments with his boot.

Kneeling on the ground, hands tied behind his back, was Brice, looking sick with fear, just as he had in my dream.

Mariah was watching him with a narrow-eyed expression. She had one beautiful leather boot resting on an overturned statue as she raised her pistol and deliberately aimed it at his head.

# CHAPTER TEN

In that hideous moment, when I saw Mariah getting ready to blow my friend to pieces, I understood what was so evil about the PODS. I understood what they'd done.

*The Dark Powers are playing with you.*

They'd studied us like a project. The creeps had studied us and taken notes and they'd figured out the things that make us who we are. Brice's compulsion to make waves, Lola's incredible ability to risk everything for love, and my desire for adventure. They'd taken everything that was deepest and best, and used them against us; planting drunken pirates and intriguing map fragments. And, like ants high on honey, we'd followed their sticky trail to Port Royal – where Mariah was waiting.

I'm not completely stupid. I did get that Mariah wasn't like, a *nice* person. But because she was Cat's granddaughter, and because she was beautiful and kind of thrillingly dangerous, I told myself it was OK.

Here in the City of the Gods I saw what she was; a human so empty, she was no longer quite human.

Mariah Darcy had sold her soul to the PODS.

As I stood watching her finger teasingly release the catch, I thought that Brice had never really stood a chance.

When you don't like yourself, when you don't know who you are, when you think you're all alone in an unfriendly universe, it leaves you open to believing all kinds of garbage. For example, that you can create a peaceful world by stealing gold to buy guns. Or that a girl pirate with a diamond tooth is the answer to your prayers.

Let's face it, Melanie, said a despairing voice inside my head, Life is basically a vast, pointless game. Even angels are just helpless pawns...

Then I felt a familiar hot-potato feeling inside my chest. Who's thinking this stuff? I thought. It's certainly not me. I'm not a pawn. The hell I am! Angelic reality is SO much bigger than this.

It was like I'd been trapped inside a lonely dark bubble all by myself and POUF! it burst and I was in a different movie.

Three Taino marksmen stepped out into the open and started firing darts. Several pirates crumpled to the ground and started snoring like stunned rhinos.

It was one of those moments when Lola and I didn't have to speak. We didn't even glance at each other. We knew Mariah was momentarily shocked so we just ran at her, jumping the pirate girl from behind, and wrestled her to the ground. I grabbed the pistol, but the vibes were so foul I dropped it in absolute revulsion.

Marohu had sliced through the ropes that bound Brice. Our buddy quickly picked up the pistol and jammed it in his belt. All three of us exchanged amazed glances. I saw baffled recognition in my friends' faces.

They're back! I thought deliriously. I rushed forward to hug them, fatally taking my eyes off Mariah.

I guess people become pirates for different reasons. I think Mariah took to piracy because when you feel that empty, not getting what you want is worse than being dead. I think after all her scheming, Maria couldn't stand to leave Coyaba empty-handed.

I saw her lunge at an exquisite Taino carving on the altar.

The statue of the weeping god had been much bigger in my dream, but its grieving expression was just the same.

"Mariah, don't!" I shouted.

The statue wasn't meant to be moved. It was part of the altar in some way. Mariah took a lethal-looking knife out of her belt and levered frantically with the blade. The blade snapped off but the damage had been done.

The ground started vibrating. There were hideous grating and rumbling sounds and a yawning crack appeared in the temple floor. I watched, paralysed, as the two jagged halves began to move apart.

Brice didn't even hesitate. He rushed forward to save her, but Mariah fell flailing into the chasm.

We stared down in horror.

A supernatural wind whipped our hair across our faces. The sky grew dark overhead.

"Quickly! We must leave!" said the old cacique.

We fled back along the tunnel. Sounds of groaning came from deep inside the earth. Blocks of stone crashed down around us.

Outside, trees writhed in this sudden hurricane as if they were trying to uproot themselves. The waters of the lake seethed and churned like a cauldron.

"Come with me," Marohu's grandfather told us. We jumped into his canoe and he paddled us fearlessly into the storm. I was too shocked to be scared. I was too shocked to feel anything at all. I had just watched a human plunge screaming to a hideous death. I thought the sound of Mariah's screams would echo through my head for ever.

There was a sudden thunderous roar. We turned our heads to see the cliff collapsing in agonising slow motion and disappear into the lake.

The old cacique watched as the sacred city of the Taino sank for ever. His eyes were clouded with pain. I saw his lips move. He was talking to someone. Not us. He'd forgotten we were even there. He was talking to one of his gods.

"They did not understand, O Cloudless One," he said softly. "But one day they will feel lost without you. They will be drawn to look for you in places of wood and water. They will remember you, and understand they must change their ways."

There's a feeling you get when you have to leave Planet Earth, no matter what's going on at that moment. Like, say someone's world has just disappeared for ever. It makes no difference. It might seem inhuman, but it's a call angels totally can't ignore.

"It's time," I whispered to my friends. I didn't want to disturb the distressed cacique while he was grieving privately with his god.

Brice and Lola were still shell-shocked, but they reached instinctively for their angel tags. As my hand closed around the platinum disc I felt the unmistakeable buzz of angelic electricity. The broken cosmic connection had been repaired.

"We're ready," I told whoever was on duty.

A whoosh of white light lit up the lakeside.

When I opened my eyes we were surrounded by delighted heavenly personnel; communications guys, maintenance people, time technicians, all talking at once and slapping us on the back.

Our clothes were filthy. Our hair was dusty and matted. Lola and Brice looked traumatised. We'd been duped by the PODS. We'd watched helplessly as the sacred city of Coyaba was destroyed, but I had brought my friends safely home.

# Chapter Eleven

For three days I couldn't even visit her. That's how ill Lola was.

It's not good for an angel to forget who she is for so long. It's not good for us to be cut off from heavenly support systems, and wander round exposed to toxic vibes. What the PODS had done to my soul-mate had burned her deep, deep inside. I didn't know if she'd ever get over it.

The first time I visited her, it was torture. Imagine me and Lola not knowing what to say to each other!

She lay there in her bed in the sanctuary, staring out at the garden, and it was like she was just waiting for me to go away and leave her alone.

I was hurt at first. Then I figured out why she couldn't talk to me.

*It hadn't happened to me.*

I never had to wake in a dark stinking hut, stiff and bruised all over from a senseless beating because I had the tiniest trace of African ancestry. I hadn't suffered such total cosmic amnesia that I believed this was who I was: a member of a subhuman species, a being regarded with such contempt that white people asked each other, in your presence, if you even had a soul.

Like I said at the beginning, my soul-mate and I were torn apart by an evil force. Who knew it would be so hard for us to find our way back?

Michael took me out to tea at Guru and told me I had to be patient. "Give her time."

"But we've been through so much together!" I said miserably. "Doesn't she realise I'm her friend by now?"

"She doesn't know what she knows," he said. "She isn't sure if she's an angel or just a slave-girl dreaming she's in heaven. Cosmic amnesia strikes to the absolute core of what you think you are."

Michael went really quiet after that and there was this feeling in the air that I just can't describe.

Back in my room, I was totally perplexed. Did he mean it had happened to him? Could a high being like Michael actually forget who and what he was? Did this kind of thing happen all the time then? Immortal beings getting trapped inside a PODS illusion, forgetting why they came to Earth, unable to find a way home?

I wondered if I'd ever met an amnesiac angel while I was alive. But how would I know? I'd have just assumed they were human, when all the time they were lying awake at nights, aching and aching inside, because something huge was missing but they couldn't remember what.

Two weeks after Lola came out of hospital, she appeared in my doorway. "Hi."

She'd been crying. She came in and curled up on a floor cushion and blew her nose. She tried to speak, but she couldn't get any words out.

"Babe, what's wrong?" I said anxiously.

Lola burst into tears. "I miss you. Isn't that stupid? You're right here in this room and I'm really missing you."

My eyes filled with tears. "I miss you too."

I didn't know what else to say. Well, I could think of plenty, but if I blurted the wrong thing, it could set us back *weeks*.

What should I do? I was practically wringing my hands. I heard myself say, "Boy, right now I could really do with a couple of lizards."

Lola stared open-mouthed, not knowing whether to laugh, cry, or give me therapy. I saw her brush away the tears from her face. "Erm, is the lizard problem new, girlfriend?" she asked cautiously, "or is it like, this shameful childhood secret you couldn't bring yourself to share until now?"

"Actually it goes back to that morning in Diego's," I told her.

"Diego's," she repeated. "That mission was something else wasn't it?"

"Just a bit."

"So what's with the lizards?" she asked curiously.

"I was having personal problems. I had to ask some lizards for help."

Lola went quiet again and I guessed she was picturing that shabby room at Diego's. "You know what was so scary?" she said suddenly. "I'd forgotten what it's like being human. I'd forgotten how lonely it feels sometimes. And when you're a slave, omigosh Melanie! I didn't trust anyone at Fruitful Vale, even the other slaves. But I really trusted Brice."

I giggled. "Boy, you were in big trouble."

She gave me a sideways glance. "The weird thing was I kind of recognised you."

I was stunned. "You did?"

"I just didn't trust what I felt. With Brice it was kind of different. You know." Lola went slightly pink.

"You really knew me?" I wanted to make sure.

"Somewhere inside I did. I just couldn't think why you wanted to know me. I'm so sorry, Mel, I just imagined you having all these like, dark motives."

My soul-mate looked tearful again so I quickly changed the subject.

"Talking of Brice. How's he doing these days? He hasn't said two words to me. Just beetles off after class to work in the library or whatever."

"How would you feel if you were him?" Lola asked softly.

"Like poo," I said. "He got Mariah totally wrong."

"He didn't. He got her right away."

I stared at her. "You think?"

"I know," she said firmly. "He knew something wasn't right. But he did that thing Brice does. He took it all on himself."

"Brice has to do it alone," I agreed. "He's the original DIY guy."

"Poor babe. His mission didn't quite work out like he hoped."

While she was talking, Lola was rolling up the cuff of her jeans so I could see she was still wearing my fraying friendship bracelet.

"It got a bit faded in Jamaica," she said in a hinting tone.

"I'll make you a new one," I said. "Just give me time."

The day after our conversation, Lola and I received invitations to attend the Angel Academy HALO awards. I know!

"How come we got invitations?" I asked my friend in amazement. "We've never been invited before."

"Maybe we've won an award?"

I knew she was just joking.

"Yeah right," I said. "That really special award you get for helping to sink a sacred city."

I felt a little pang for Brice. He'd tried so hard. Life can be really unfair.

The HALO ceremony was ridiculously short notice, plus we were revising for exams, so I didn't even have time to buy clothes. I had to wear that glittery grey dress I bought the first time I went shopping with Lola. My soul-mate wore a similar dress in pale gold and we put each other's hair up.

We examined ourselves in her mirror.

"Hey we look hot, girl!" she grinned.

When we arrived, the hall was packed out with agents and trainees, all dressed up to the nines.

All around us kids were spouting advanced angel jargon. You know that type who love talking in initials? DS for Dark Studies and TTs for time technicians.

Lola fished out a pen from her bag and wrote C.W.O.T on her hand. "Complete Waste of TIme," she whispered. We both sniggered like naughty children.

Then I saw something I never thought I'd see in this universe.

I nudged Lola. "Look who's sitting across the aisle."

"How DID they get that boy in a suit?" she said wonderingly.

I giggled. "From the look on his face he's wishing he was back in the Hell dimensions."

The ceremony kicked off with the usual speeches about teamwork, yadda yadda, then people were called up to receive their awards.

It was warm in the hall, and I was tired from staying up revising. I kept almost nodding off. Now and then there'd be a burst of applause and I'd jump awake guiltily and realise where I was.

Suddenly there was a huge outbreak of clapping and cheering.

I practically leapt out of my seat. "What's happening?"

Lola was looking stunned. "We won an award!"

"Don't be stupid," I told her.

"I mean it. We won!"

My voice shot up an octave. "What the sassafras for?"

"I'm not sure. I think it was 'Brilliant teamwork under unusual adversity'," she said.

Everybody was craning round, wondering why we weren't going up to get our trophies.

Mr Allbright stood up. "They're in shock," he told the audience. A ripple of laughter went round the hall.

I followed Lola self-consciously to the front. My knees had totally turned to water.

Brice was waiting for us, looking like some alarming stranger in his suit. We all filed up the steps and there was Michael smiling at us.

Some strange Agency type I had never seen in my life made a speech about how we were the finest example of something or other he'd seen in such young trainees.

Apparently we were supposed to say something. Unfortunately, I'm utterly phobic about public speaking. I completely froze. Brice just stood glowering at the audience. Not the most shining example of angelic teamwork, you have to admit. Lola saved the day luckily. She stepped up to the mike, beaming and looking absolutely divine in her glittery gold dress, thanking everyone for supporting us while we were going through our ordeal.

"But most of all," she said breathlessly, "I want to thank my team-mates, Mel and Br—"

Brice turned white and bolted out of the hall.

"Better go after him," Michael whispered in my ear.

I found him outside the building, practically in tears.

"Hey, you're missing your big moment," I said. "What's up?"

Brice shook his head. "I've been asking myself the same question. I think I got scared."

"Of an *award* ceremony! After the stuff you've seen?"

He wiped his eyes, trying to laugh. "It wasn't stage fright, darling. It was more like that old Taino guy watching his city go under the water. Like my entire life was ending or something."

"WHY? This is just the beginning. You wanted that award, that's—"

"I *know*," he said angrily. "Look, this is humiliatingly cheesy, but maybe I'm not sure I deserve it.

"Why ever not?" I said. "You didn't know who you were but you had all these like, amazing *principles*. You even tried to save Mariah, when I'd have been tempted to—"

"I know, I know, OK? Spare me. So am I like, a really good boy now?" Brice peered down at his suit in a kind of horror. "Because, be honest, sweetheart. Is this really me?"

I felt like slapping him. "This is ridiculous, man! Why are you so hung up about a stupid suit?"

"Because..." Brice struggled for words. "I knew how to do *twisted*, OK? It worked for me. I'm not sure I can hack that other stuff."

"I don't see a tragedy here," I said firmly. "I don't even see a teeny weeny problem."

"You don't?"

I patted his shoulder. "Absolutely not. You can be twisted if that's your style. You can be that twisted angel boy who goes around in a stinky Astral Garbage T-shirt. You can be that dark dangerous stinky teenage angel."

Brice perked up. "Dangerous? Ooh, sounds promising!"

I swatted him with my sparkly clutch bag. "Come on. Let's go and rescue poor Lola from the AWTIIs."

He looked blank.

"Angels Who Talk In Initials!" I grinned.

We started walking back.

But I could see Brice was still terrified, so I did that thing I still occasionally find myself doing, when things get heavy. That airhead thing.

"Incidentally," I giggled. "You owe me BIG time, angel boy! Do you have ANY idea what a nightmare you put me through?"

Brice looked bewildered. "For making you enter the HALO awards?"

"No, dirtbag! For making me wear a corset!"

Read the **ANGELS UNLIMITED** book that started it all!

# Winging it

Mel is on a mission...

Mel isn't your average angel. How would you feel if you wound up in a posh Angel Academy, learning about halos and teamwork, when all you're really interested in is shopping and boys? Her angel wardrobe is drop-dead gorgeous, admittedly. But hey, if she's an angel, she should look divine, right? It's just all the work that really freaks her out. But when Mel goes on her first angelic assignment to wartime London, she realises that maybe, for the first time, she's found something she's actually good at...

Join Mel in her first cosmic adventure!

*An imprint of* HarperCollins*Publishers*

www.angelsunlimited.co.uk

Another brilliant read in the *ANGELS UNLIMITED* series...

# calling the Shots

## Look out, Hollywood...

Mel loves being an angel – who wouldn't? She lives
in Paradise, has the best friends in the world, can
shop till she drops and gets to travel the universe.
But when Mel is sent on a solo assignment to
America in the 1920s, she has more than a touch of
stage-fright. It may look exciting in the movies, but
life is dangerous in honky-tonk tinseltown, even for
someone as angelic as Mel!

Join Mel in her fourth cosmic adventure!

An imprint of HarperCollins*Publishers*

www.angelsunlimited.co.uk

The sixth book in the fantastic **ANGELS UNLIMITED** series...

# Fighting Fit

Mel gets the gladiator groove!

Mel's big-time crush Orlando's got a lot on his mind. So when he puts together a team of angel volunteers to go to Ancient Rome, Mel signs up. Hey, it's a chance to get close to the boy of her dreams! But in the cruel, decadent world of the Roman Empire's last days, her fantasies crumble. Who is the mysterious girl gladiator Orlando is trying so hard to protect? Is his concern purely professional, or is it something more?

Join Mel in her sixth cosmic adventure!

*An imprint of* HarperCollins*Publishers*

www.angelsunlimited.co.uk

Coming soon in the brilliant **ANGELS UNLIMITED** series...

# Budding Star

Mel travels to ancient Japan...

🔖 *An imprint of HarperCollinsPublishers*

www.angelsunlimited.co.uk

# Order Form

To order direct from the publishers, just make a list of the titles you want and fill in the form below:

Name ...................................................................................

Address ..............................................................................

..........................................................................................

..........................................................................................

Send to: Dept 6, HarperCollins Publishers Ltd, Westerhill Road, Bishopbriggs, Glasgow G64 2QT.

Please enclose a cheque or postal order to the value of the cover price, plus:

UK & BFPO: Add £1.00 for the first book, and 25p per copy for each additional book ordered.

Overseas and Eire: Add £2.95 service charge. Books will be sent by surface mail but quotes for airmail despatch will be given on request.

A 24-hour telephone ordering service is available to holders of Visa, MasterCard, Amex or Switch cards on 0141- 772 2281.

*An imprint of* HarperCollins*Publishers*